REASON TO DECEIVE

Justine Farrell is delighted when her friend Dee Sullivan invites her to accompany her to the Spanish town of Javea for a holiday in a luxury villa. Justine is instantly attracted to the occupant of the neighbouring villa, the handsome Cal Douglas, who says he is researching a book on Spanish history. But as the holiday proceeds, and events move out of Justine's control, she soon realizes that Cal is not what he seems.

Books by Karen West
in the Linford Romance Library:

HAMILTON'S FOLLY
THE MUSIC OF LOVE

KAREN WEST

REASON
TO DECEIVE

Complete and Unabridged

LINFORD
Leicester

First published in Great Britain in 1993 by
Robert Hale Limited, London

First Linford Edition
published 2000
by arrangement with
Robert Hale Limited, London

British Library CIP Data

West, Karen
  Reason to deceive.—Large print ed.—
  Linford romance library
  1. Love stories
  2. Large type books
  I. Title
  823.9'14 [F]

  ISBN 0–7089–5639–4

Published by
F. A. Thorpe (Publishing) Ltd.
Anstey, Leicestershire

Set by Words & Graphics Ltd.
Anstey, Leicestershire
Printed and bound in Great Britain by
T. J. International Ltd., Padstow, Cornwall

This book is printed on acid-free paper

In Memory of Derek
who so loved Javea

1

The road out of Javea wound torturously through wooded hills and as the taxi chugged up the steep incline Justine Farrell felt a tingle of excitement. It was her first visit to Spain and when they had landed at Alicante she had been disappointed at the barrenness of the terrain but as they had travelled up the coast the arid landscape had given way to lush vegetation and steep terraces of dark-leafed orange groves.

'It seems to be rather a way from the town,' observed her friend Dee Sullivan as they climbed between thick pine trees their branches spread wide like umbrellas, unlike English pines. 'We'll have to see if we can hire a car while we're here,' she added.

They caught glimpses of sumptuous villas behind ornamental stone walls, splashes of bright colour from exotic flowering shrubs. Then just when Justine was wondering whenever the taxi was going to stop climbing it scrunched to a halt before stone gateposts. A blue and white mosaic plaque on one of the posts clearly stated Las Bellotas in ornate black lettering. Leaving Dee working out the correct amount of pesetas to pay the driver, Justine began to lift their luggage from the boot.

The car turned round in the driveway and hurtled away down the hill with a cheery wave from the driver while Justine staggered forward under the weight of their cases. But as she caught sight of the villa which was to be home for the next ten days, she stopped. Slowly she set down the bags and stared.

'Oh, Dee,' she breathed as the other girl joined her. 'Look at this. It's lovely.'

The villa was white with a roof of ridged tiles the colour of old rose. One wall was rounded reminding Justine of the keep to a small castle while the main entrance at the top of a flight of tiled steps was tucked away under a large verandah its roof supported by high archways and its floor bounded by fancy black wrought iron railings. The same railings or grills covered the shuttered Gothic-style windows. A delicate flowering jasmine had crept up the walls its tendrils entwined through the railings while terracotta pots of geraniums provided vivid splashes of colour against the stark whiteness of the walls.

Beyond the villa the dry rocky earth of the garden yielded several hardy cacti while behind that they could see a tiled patio and the sparkling blue of a swimming pool.

'Oh, yes,' breathed Dee, pushing her sunglasses onto the top of her head. 'I can't wait to get into that water.'

Justine nodded and pushed back her long dark hair already damp from the heat. 'Let's get these bags inside first.'

They'd started to pick up the luggage

again when a sudden shout made them pause. A man in the next villa was leaning over the wall.

'Hi, there. Can I give you a hand?' Not waiting for an answer he moved swiftly through his gateway and joined them.

'That's very kind of you . . . ' Justine began then paused as he laughed.

'That's good,' he said.

'What is?'

'You're English . . . '

'Yes . . . '

'My Spanish isn't very good . . . and there again my German's not up to much either.' He held out his hand and Dee stepped forward and grasped it. He looked nice, thought Justine. He was wearing a pair of the shortest denim shorts imaginable and white canvas shoes. He was fairly tall, loose limbed with tawny coloured hair that swept back from his forehead in an attractive widow's peak. His eyes were hidden behind dark glasses but she judged him to be about thirty. His body was only lightly tanned making Justine think that he couldn't have been in Spain for very long but the hairs on his chest, arms and legs had turned a deep golden bronze. She was still thinking how attractive he looked when he turned from Dee and held out his hand to her. 'Welcome to Las Bellotas,' he said and his voice was pleasant. 'I'm your temporary neighbour, the name's Douglas — Calvin Douglas or Cal to my friends.'

'Pleased to meet you,' breathed Justine feeling even hotter than she had in the taxi. 'I'm Justine Farrell and this is Dee Sullivan.'

'How long are you here for?' he asked as he picked up the two large suitcases leaving them to cope with their hand luggage.

'Just ten days,' replied Dee as they followed him across the garden to the verandah steps. 'And you? Have you just arrived as well?'

'Uh, no, I've been here a while,' he replied.

'Lucky you, how much longer have you got?'

'I'm not certain yet.' They had reached the top of the steps by then and he'd set the cases down while Dee fumbled in her handbag for the keys. 'I'm not really on holiday. Although I suppose you could call it a working holiday — I'm doing some research.'

'What a fantastic place to work,' said Justine as she turned and looked towards the mountains in the distance and the plunging valley beneath them. 'But tell me,' she turned back to him curiously, 'what is the noise we can hear?' She'd noticed the high pitched ringing as soon as they'd stepped from the taxi.

He grinned. 'You'll have to get used to that, I'm afraid. It's the crickets or cicadas as the locals call them — they live in the pines and they keep that racket up for most of the time. Don't worry, you hardly notice it after a while. And if it does bother you too much, you can look forward to when it stops, because it's bliss then.'

By this time Dee had found the key and had unlocked the front door which swung open to reveal a spacious living room with a ceramic tiled floor, pine beams and a huge stone fireplace. The furniture was cane, beautifully crafted and padded with pink and green floral cushions while deeper pink curtains hung at the two windows. Dried flowers added colour, arranged in tall vases of Spanish pottery and twisted pieces of driftwood bleached white by the hot sun dotted the hearth. The cool white walls were bare save for wrought iron wall lights and a few prints of timeless Spanish scenes.

The girls exclaimed in delight and while their neighbour carried in their cases they explored further discovering a fitted pine kitchen and two bedrooms, each cool with shuttered windows, mosquito nets and beds covered with cream Spanish lace. The bathroom was luxurious with a champagne tinted suite and matching tiles.

'There's everything we could possibly need,' said Justine.

Calvin Douglas grinned, took off his sunglasses and for a moment his eyes met hers. They were an unusual colour, not green and not quite brown, in fact they appeared almost golden, in keeping with his tawny hair which he wore slightly longer than was fashionable so that it waved into the nape of his neck. The effect was almost leonine, very masculine, then Justine realised he was looking at her in an amused, questioning fashion.

As she looked quickly away he said, 'I'd say you have everything except food and drink.' He glanced round the kitchen his eyes coming to rest on Dee as she stood on a stool and struggled to open the window. She was wearing tight denims that hugged her hips and a white shirt, its collar turned up below her cropped golden hair. Dee always managed to look stylish thought Justine as she ruefully glanced down at the cool, practical cotton skirt and top that she'd chosen to wear for travelling.

The two girls were in fact a perfect foil for each other, Dee, tall and blue eyed with golden blonde hair and fair skin and Justine, a little shorter but very slim with long legs, an olive complexion, lustrous dark eyes and a mass of dark hair.

At that moment however all Justine was concerned with was the fact that she was feeling hot and sticky and was longing to take a shower or better still a dip in the pool.

'Talking of supplies,' said Dee as she climbed from the stool, holding out her hand for Calvin Douglas to assist her, 'We were wondering if we could hire a car.'

'Well, you could,' he replied slowly, 'but it's expensive, about a hundred pounds a week.'

'That's out then,' said Justine swiftly. 'Our budget won't stretch to that. Maybe there's a bus we can use?' she asked hopefully.

'I wouldn't count on it,' he grinned.

'But I've got a car, I go down to the town most days, I could always give you a lift.'

'Oh we couldn't possibly . . . ' began Justine only to be cut short by Dee.

'That's very kind of you . . . Mr . . . er . . . Douglas. We might be very glad to take you up on your offer.'

'Right, that's settled then and the name's Cal.'

'Of course,' Dee smiled at him beneath her dark eyelashes and Justine found herself wishing for the umpteenth time that she was as outgoing as her friend, especially where men were concerned.

'I'll leave you to get yourselves sorted out then in a couple of hours I'll drive you down to the town so that you can get some supplies.'

'Thank you,' said Justine as Dee wandered outside. 'That's kind of you . . . Cal. We never expected to have a good neighbour as part of the deal.'

'What deal's that?'

'The holiday,' she explained. 'We've been loaned the villa by some friends.'

'That's the sort of friends to have.'

'They're friends of Dee's actually. I don't even know them. I've just come along for the ride.'

'I'm glad you did.' He smiled at her and her heart missed a beat. 'It'll be nice to have company. It was getting lonely around here.'

'Aren't all the villas occupied?' asked Justine turning to look through the open door where Dee could be seen leaning over the balcony. Beyond her the rooftops of other villas further down the valley were just visible.

'Some of them are,' he replied, 'mostly with retired British who've come out here to live, but the other properties are used exclusively for holidays, some only as little as a couple of times a year.' He glanced at his wristwatch. 'I must be going, I'll see you girls later.' With a wave of his hand he strolled down the steps and across the garden.

'He's really nice,' said Justine as Dee came back into the villa.

'Smitten, are we?' said Dee teasingly.

'Of course not. But I think we're jolly lucky to have him next door.'

'Hmm, let's hope he doesn't make a nuisance of himself,' said Dee.

'You were the one who took him up on his offer of lifts in his car,' Justine put in swiftly.

'That was too good a chance to turn down,' Dee grinned.

'So you'll use his services as a chauffeur but you don't want him hanging around,' said Justice in exasperation. 'Honestly Dee, that's typical of you. Lead them on, then give them the cold shoulder.'

By this time they'd got back into the kitchen and Dee opened her bag taking out two cans of coke and tossing one to Justine, then growing serious she said, 'Talking of men, I've got a confession to make, Jus.'

'What sort of confession?' Justine looked up swiftly. Dee was frequently unpredictable and nothing she did really surprised Justine. Pulling the ring on her can Dee eased herself onto one of the breakfast stools.

'I had another reason for coming here,' she said tipping her head back and taking a mouthful of coke. 'Ugh, that's warm,' she complained.

'I'm not surprised, it's been in your bag all the way from the airport,' replied Justine. 'So what was this other reason? Would I be right in assuming it has something to do with a man?'

Dee grinned. 'The trouble with you is that you know me too well.' Then as Justine waited she grew serious again and a troubled expression crossed her features. 'This one's special, Justine, he really is. I've come out here to find him.'

Justine stared at her in silence then shaking her head she said stiffly, 'I'm sorry, Dee, I didn't realise there was an ulterior motive to this holiday.'

'I can't see what difference it makes,' replied Dee.

'Won't I cramp your style? I'm not too keen on playing gooseberry.'

'Oh Jus, it won't be like that, honest, and after all, we are still getting ten days rent free in a luxury villa — ulterior motive or not!'

'But it's so unlike you to go chasing after a man. Let's face it, it's usually the other way round,' observed Justine silently recalling the number of men who'd been after Dee in the past and who had usually been ditched for their pains.

'I'm not chasing after him!' denied Dee pushing her fingers through her short golden hair. 'It's not like that.'

Justine sighed. 'That's certainly what it sounds like.' She threw her friend a puzzled glance. 'So what's so special about this one?'

Dee shrugged helplessly. 'I don't know — he was just different and . . .' she hesitated, 'I know this is going to sound crazy, but I have this feeling something has happened to him. I haven't heard from him, you see.'

Justine frowned. 'How long did you spend together?'

'Just over a week.' A defiant note had crept into Dee's voice. 'I know what you're thinking, but you're quite wrong.'

'But why do you think something might have happened to him?' persisted Justine.

'Because he promised he would be in touch.'

'And how long ago was that?'

'Nearly two months . . .'

'Oh Dee . . . it sounds like the classic holiday romance . . .'

'Except that neither of us were on holiday . . . at least, he wasn't, but I'd taken a few days off for Cowes week.'

'What was his name?'

'Ramon, Ramon Amador.'

'So what do you know about him?'

'Not very much actually,' admitted Dee pulling a face. 'Apart from the fact that he works for a wine merchant who have their headquarters in Valencia.'

'But you know he lives in Javea?'

'Not really, I only know he comes from this region.'

'So you don't have very much to go on?'

Dee shook her head then slipping off the stool she said, 'That's true, but I was toying with the idea of coming to Spain to find him when Diana Galloway came into the office. I haven't seen her for years then when we got talking she told me she had this villa, honestly Jus, it seemed like some sort of sign. Anyway, we had lunch, then she said the villa was empty for these ten days and asked me if I'd like to come out here and bring a friend.'

'And you thought of me,' said Justine aware there was a cryptic note in her voice.

'Yes, I did. You've been moping around for long enough. I bet you haven't been out with anyone since that wretched Gary went off the scene and besides, I thought you might have liked the idea of a few days in the sun,' said Dee defensively.

Justine stared at her then seeing her friend's hurt expression she said, 'I'm sorry Dee. Of course I did. I was delighted when you asked me. It was just that for a moment I thought you were going to be off with this Spanish guy and leaving me to my own devices.'

'Chance to be a fine thing,' muttered Dee then with a sudden grin she added, 'Besides, even if I did, if you play your cards right you could score with our neighbour. I saw the way he was looking at you.'

'Every time I looked at him he was looking at you!' Justine sniffed but her heart had began to beat faster at Dee's words. What her friend had said had been true, she hadn't been out with anyone since her relationship with Gary Thompson had ended, she hadn't wanted to. But now, she had to admit there was something very intriguing about Cal Douglas.

'Listen, Justine,' said Dee a little

later as they carried their cases through to the bedrooms, 'I promise I won't let this issue with Ramon dominate our holiday, we're here to have a good time and another reason I asked you was because we haven't seen much of each other lately and I thought this would be an opportunity to catch up. I admit I would like to find Ramon but I won't let that interfere with the things we'd planned to do.'

When Justine remained silent she went on, 'I know you think I'm mad, and I know I could be in for a nasty shock when I do find him, but I'm sorry, Jus, I have to try.' She shrugged. 'I've got it bad this time, I can't get him out of my mind.'

'Oh, Dee, I'm sorry. I didn't realise it was that bad.' Justine stared at her friend in concern struck by the unexpected note of despair in her voice. 'I'll do all I can to help you. Things might not be as you imagined when you do find him but . . . ' she trailed off uncertainly.

Dee shrugged then seemed to brighten. 'Right, that's enough of that,' she said, unzipping her jeans, 'Let's get this holiday on the road.' As she spoke she unbuttoned her shirt, tossed it onto the bed then struggled free from her jeans. She wasn't wearing a bra, and pausing only to rummage in her case, she pulled on bright blue bikini briefs. She stopped in the doorway and glancing back at Justine who was still fully dressed she said, 'Come on, aren't you coming for a swim?'

'Yes, of course, but I thought we were going to unpack first.'

'That can wait. I need to cool off.' She tossed her hair back from her face and her large hooped earrings glittered in the sunlight that filtered through the shutters.

'Aren't you going to wear the top to that?' Justine nodded at her briefs. 'Don't forget we have a neighbour.'

'I hadn't forgotten,' said Dee wickedly, then with a pout she picked up the skimpy bikini bra, covered her firm high breasts and fastened it. 'I suppose I'd better wear it — but just because he's next door I'm not going to miss out on topless sun-bathing nor midnight skinny-dipping.'

'Honestly, Dee you're the limit,' said Justine with a laugh then turning to her case she began hunting for her own bikini.

Dee wandered from the room but before she could have got much further than the verandah she was back.

Justine looked up as she stepped out of her skirt. 'What's the matter?'

'Talking of our neighbour,' said Dee slowly. 'There's something familiar about him. I'm sure I've seen him somewhere before.'

'I haven't,' said Justine firmly, thinking to herself that if she had she would have been sure to have remembered him. It wasn't every day that she came across someone as attractive as Cal Douglas.

Dee shook her head thoughtfully. 'I can't for the life of me think where I've seen him. Not to worry it may come to me later, the important thing now is to get into that glorious water.'

With that she was gone leaving Justine to fasten her scarlet bikini and follow her outside into the hot Spanish sunshine.

2

Justine's bikini was a perfect contrast for her dark hair and olive skin which tanned easily, whereas Dee who was fair skinned burnt quickly and had to take care in the hot sun.

As she padded through the villa the coolness of the marble tiles struck her feet but as she stepped outside, the burning heat on the steps hit her and she ran towards the pool. Dee was floating on her back her face turned to the sun. As Justine approached she raised her head.

'Come on in, it's fabulous,' she called.

Justine needed no second bidding and after testing the water with her toe she climbed down the blue and yellow ceramic steps into the cool depths. After the intense heat of the sun the temperature of the water took her breath away but as her body became acclimatised she struck out and had soon completed several laps. The water soon felt warm and the girls abandoned the serious business of swimming and basked in the sun allowing the water to gently lap their bodies.

'You can see next door from here,' said Dee suddenly. 'It's a huge villa.'

Justine opened her eyes and looked in the direction where Cal had gone. Great masses of pink and purple bougainvillaea tumbled over the wall that divided their pool from the villa next door. From their own villa they had been unable to see the neighbouring property but the pool afforded a different angle and quite clearly they could see what indeed appeared to be a large and luxurious villa. It too was painted white with rose tinted ridge tiles on the roof while between the flowering shrubs could be seen tantalising glimpses of a terrace or patio dotted with sun-loungers.

'Do you think it's his?' asked Dee

shielding her eyes from the fierce sunlight to get a better look.

'I wouldn't have thought so,' replied Justine doubtfully. 'He spoke as if he was simply staying there.'

'He could still own it,' Dee observed. 'You heard what he said about people who owned these places only coming for a few weeks of the year.'

'That's true,' agreed Justine. 'But he also said something about a working holiday — research, wasn't it? I wonder what sort?'

'How about research into having a good time in a setting of utter luxury?' Dee laughed and ducked under water again then surfacing and flicking the water from her eyes she added, 'If that's what he's doing then I'll volunteer to help!' She closed her eyes and lifted her face to the sun again. 'You know something, Jus, this is perfect. I really need a holiday. I haven't had any time off at all this year.'

'What about Cowes week?'

Dee was silent for a moment and

Justine wished she hadn't mentioned it then her friend sighed. 'Believe it or not but Cowes week was hard work.'

'Really? I thought you said that was where you met . . . what's his name — Ramon?'

She nodded. 'It was, but I was crewing for my uncle. It's been Admiral's Cup year and he was racing his company's yacht. It all went wrong because my uncle was taken ill and he left me in charge of the yacht while the rest of the crew lived it up in Cowes. It turned out to be only his hiatus hernia playing up but we thought it might have been his heart so it was all a bit frantic.'

'Until you met Ramon.'

Dee sighed. 'Yes, until I met Ramon. Since then nothing's quite been the same.'

'So was he at Cowes for the racing?'

'Good heavens no. Well, not directly. He was there for Cowes week but he wasn't involved with the racing.'

'Like a good many others,' observed Justine drily.

Dee managed a smile. 'His firm was involved with this year's sponsorship.'

Both girls fell silent then Justine said, 'Couldn't you have contacted him through his firm?'

'I tried but I couldn't find an address in the UK. I did try their company office in Valencia but I couldn't seem to make them understand who I was talking about. It was a case of their English being bad and my Spanish being non-existent but it should all be easier now that I'm in the country.'

Justine didn't answer, she still felt the whole thing sounded dubious. Ramon quite likely didn't want to be found, probably he was married and the last person he would want to see would be Dee Sullivan. It had however been Dee's attitude that had surprised Justine, for it was so out of character.

The two girls had been friends all their lives in spite of the fact that they came from different backgrounds. Dee's father was the managing director of an aircraft factory and the family were relatively well off, while Justine's mother had been widowed when Justine was a child and life for them had never been easy. Justine glanced at her friend who once again was floating on her back and found herself hoping that she wasn't lining up a lot of heartache.

At that moment a movement beyond the wall caught her eye and as the sun's rays flashed on some sharp object she realised that someone was standing on the terrace. She blinked in the strong light but when she looked again the terrace was empty. Had she imagined it or had Cal Douglas been watching them? Or could it even have been someone else? Maybe he had a companion with him at the villa — perhaps a woman? At the thought she felt a stab of disappointment and she glanced at Dee again who apparently had seen nothing. Then all such notions flew from her mind.

'Dee,' she said sharply. 'You're burning already! For goodness' sake put some cream on your nose!'

With a wail Dee flipped over and splashed to the steps, hoisted herself out of the pool then ran indoors leaving the darker skinned Justine to follow more leisurely.

True to his word, a couple of hours later Cal Douglas was back, this time in a small white Renault which he backed onto the short driveway. The girls had showered after their swim and had changed into shorts and suntops but their hair was still wet.

'It'll soon dry in this heat,' said Dee as she automatically pulled the seat forward for Justine to climb into the back then she sat beside Cal.

'Well, yours might,' Justine replied. 'Mine will take a little longer.' Her long dark hair was her one source of vanity.

'Did you enjoy your swim?' asked Cal as they began the steep descent into the valley.

'It was bliss,' said Dee while something in Cal's tone convinced Justine that it

28

had indeed been him watching them from his terrace.

'Where are you girls from?' he went on as he expertly negotiated the sharp bends in the road.

'The Isle of Wight,' replied Dee absent-mindedly as she gazed out of the window.

'Really?' For a moment he took his eyes from the road in surprise.

'Yes really.' Dee laughed then said, 'Why is it that people always react in that fashion? I'm sure there wouldn't be the same impact if we said, Milton Keynes or Scunthorpe or even London, but the minute you say you're from the Isle of Wight people stare at you as if you're some sort of oddity.'

'I've always put it down to envy,' said Justine.

'That was more my reaction,' said Cal. 'I come from London, and the only time I get that sort of reaction is when I tell an American where I come from.'

They all laughed then Dee threw

him a sidelong glance, 'What part of London are you from?'

'Streatham.' His reply was curt as if he didn't wish to discuss it any further.

By that time they had reached the foot of the hills and the main road into Javea and as they turned left, Justine suddenly said, 'Look, Dee there's that mountain again, the one shaped like an elephant.'

'That's Montgo,' said Cal. 'It's something of a landmark around here. I see you've already noticed the elephant resemblance or did someone point it out to you?'

'Yes, the taxi-driver did,' said Dee.

'It really does look like an elephant, doesn't it?' mused Justine. 'There's its trunk stretching right along that ridge and look, it even has an eye.'

'That eye is actually a large cave,' explained Cal as he took a right hand turning and they plunged into a warren of unmade roads through acres of orange groves.

'You seem well informed about the area,' said Dee and when Cal shrugged, Justine leaned forward and said, 'Is it all part of your research?'

He hesitated then said. 'Yes, that's right. I had to find out a great deal about the area.'

Justine wanted to ask him more but he gave her no chance. 'I was wondering why you girls felt the need to come to Spain when you've just spent the summer on the Isle of Wight.'

'That's simple,' said Dee quickly. 'The sun's hotter, here.'

In that instant Justine guessed that Dee didn't want Cal to know the real reason they were in Javea. 'Actually, we've been lucky, we've had a good summer at home,' she broke in swiftly, 'but it's always nice to go somewhere for a break. Besides I like to see how other people live.'

'Have you been to Spain before?' asked Cal glancing in his mirror.

Justine briefly allowed her eyes to meet his. Then she shook her head.

'No, but Dee has, haven't you, Dee?'

She nodded and Cal glanced at her. 'Have you been to Javea before?'

'No, Marbella. I was crewing on board a yacht.'

He gave a low whistle. 'I'm impressed.'

Justine sank back into her seat. Dee always stole the limelight. As long as she could remember, Dee was always the one who generated the most interest, especially with men, because she was the one who was glamorous and who had done exciting things. And even now when Dee was so wrapped up in finding Ramon she seemed to be commanding Cal's attention in a way that Justine could never manage.

The little car continued to hurtle through the orange groves where the green unripened fruit hung in thick clusters amidst the dark shiny leaves. Swarthy local men were working in the groves some driving tiny tractors that looked like mechanised lawn mowers while others wielded rakes or scythes.

'Their siesta's over now,' said Cal.

'You'll find everyone's back at work, the shops close between one and four but they'll all be open again now until about eight o'clock.'

As Cal was speaking Justine found herself staring at the back of his head fascinated by the thick tawny hair that touched the collar of the shirt he was now wearing over his shorts. She wondered if he was a writer and if that was why he was engaged in research, or maybe he was some sort of scientist. He drove them to the old part of the town through narrow alleyways between ancient buildings of Moorish architecture, past mysterious stone archways and flights of steps their stones worn smooth, and half hidden doorways covered by wrought iron grills. They passed the bank, the post office, and a circle of seats in the centre of the road where old men congregated to gossip and drink brandy. A young policewoman on traffic duty waved them on through the town to the port where enormous date palms and rubber trees fringed the road and beyond they glimpsed the sparkling blue of the Mediterranean.

Eventually Cal stopped the car, pulling up at a food store. 'You should be able to get all you need in here,' he said.

They stocked up with groceries, fruit and vegetables, wine and bottles of mineral water. Cal made several purchases of his own then as they were stowing everything into the boot of the car Dee remembered she wanted a certain brand of shampoo and went back into the shop leaving Justine with Cal. They sat on a low wall and in spite of the fact that it was late afternoon the sun still burned fiercely on their bare limbs.

'Do you sail as well?' he asked casually nodding towards the shop where they could see Dee's golden head as she moved around inside.

'Good heavens, no. I've been out with Dee and her family on the Solent but I've never really learnt to sail.'

'Is it her father she crews for?'

'No, her uncle. He's skipper of a large yacht, owned by his company I think . . . although her father does sail as well. They owned a smaller boat and Dee used to sail that but I think her father sold it some while ago. She was only saying today that she was crewing for her uncle at Cowes this year.'

'Do her family live at Cowes?'

'No, at Bembridge but Dee works for a yacht broker's in Cowes.' She glanced at Cal and saw that a deep frown had creased his forehead as he watched Dee in the shop. She found herself wishing that he was as interested in her as he appeared to be in Dee.

Almost as if he read her thoughts he turned slightly and said, 'And what about you? Where do you live?'

'I live in a village called Seaview.'

'Have you known Dee very long?'

'We've been friends since we were children, we learnt to ride at the same stables.' She threw him a glance from beneath her lashes and wished that the sight of his bare legs with their covering of bronze hair didn't affect her so much. She took a deep breath. 'And what about you?' she asked hoping the question came out casually.

'Me?' He frowned.

'Yes, we know very little about you, except that your name is Cal and you come from Streatham.' She giggled. 'It makes you sound like a contestant on 'Blind Date'.'

'I'm sorry?' He gave her a puzzled look and she realised he'd never heard of the quiz show.

'It's a show on the telly,' she began then catching sight of his polite expression she muttered, 'Oh, never mind . . . how about telling me about your research?'

He shrugged. 'There's not a lot to tell.'

'I'm sure there must be, it sounds intriguing.' Out of the corner of her eye she could see Dee coming out of the shop. 'What is it exactly that you're researching?'

'Spanish history.'

She stared at him. 'But that's fascinating.' When he remained silent she went on, 'Are you an historian or a writer?'

He stood up as Dee reached the car and as he moved forward to open the door, he said, 'A bit of both really. I'm compiling a book on the history of Spain.'

'But that's marvellous.' Justine stared at him as if she couldn't believe her ears. 'I adore history.'

'Do you know,' Dee announced loudly breaking into their conversation, 'I tried for three different brands of shampoo and they didn't have any of them, I had to settle for this,' she held up a plastic bottle, 'my hair will probably turn green with the sun and the chlorine in the pool. You'd think they'd stock every brand wouldn't you?'

Cal smiled and held the door open for her. 'You were lucky to have the choice you did,' he remarked.

They climbed into the car and as Cal turned the key in the ignition Justine leaned forward between the front seats, 'Dee, Cal is a writer and historian, he's writing a book on Spanish history.'

'Well, that's right up your street, isn't it?' Dee sniffed. 'I suppose I shall have the pair of you going on about boring old history. Just my luck, one of you's bad enough, but two!'

'What do you mean?' Cal turned his head slightly.

'Well, Justine's potty about history. Always has been. Don't know what she finds so interesting. It bores me to death. You'd think she'd get enough of it where she works but no, she even has to belong to a History Society.'

'And where do you work?' Once again Cal's gaze met Justine's in the driving mirror and this time she felt her heart give a crazy lift. It was very rare she met a man with the same interest as her and one whom she found physically attractive. The last one had been Gary and that had all been over a long time ago.

'I work at Osborne House,' she said quietly. 'I'm personal assistant to the chief custodian.' She said it with the warm little glow of pride she always felt when anyone asked about her work.

'Osborne House?' he said slowly.

'You know,' chimed in Dee. 'Where Queen Victoria lived. It's our one and only stately home.'

'Have you been to the Isle of Wight?' Dee asked Cal as gathering speed they headed away from the port.

'Only once,' he replied briefly. 'When I was child; a family holiday in a guest house in Shanklin.'

'So it's not on the island where I've seen you before,' mused Dee.

'What did you say?' Justine watched as Cal threw Dee a startled glance.

'I thought I knew you from some-where. As soon as I met you your face seemed familiar.' She shrugged her bare shoulders, 'but maybe I was mistaken, unless perhaps we've met in London. I go up to town frequently, perhaps we went to the same party or something.'

'I don't think so, I would have remembered you.' He laughed, and Justine wished he would say something like that to her. She sighed and looked out of the window.

They appeared to have entered the valley by a different route, a smooth stretch of dual carriageway which took them for several miles between acres of vines thick with luscious golden grapes. Then as they turned off the road onto an unadopted lane they passed luxurious houses tucked away behind high walls most set with black iron gates. Large dogs, Dobermann and Alsatians guarded some of the houses and occasionally they glimpsed big expensive cars in the driveways.

'Are they holiday villas?' asked Justine innocently.

Cal laughed. 'No, not in the way you mean, they belong to wealthy Spanish families who live in town during the week and come here at weekends.

Some come from as far away as Madrid or Valencia.'

Justine saw that Dee was looking curiously at the houses now and she guessed that she was wondering about Ramon and where he lived. While they had been in the town she had also noticed that Dee had spent much of her time not looking at the architecture or places of interest but at the faces of local people as if she expected any moment to see the one face she wanted to see. Justine thought it was like looking for a needle in a haystack although she didn't say as much to Dee. They had left the houses in the valley far behind and climbed their way to Las Bellotas but this time they approached it from the opposite side and had a glimpse of one corner of Cal's villa. Creeping vines and busy-lizzies fringed the terrace which was shaded by a large date palm, while purple bougainvillaea tumbled over the white outer wall and scarlet poinsettias dotted the marbled steps.

'Gorgeous place you have there, Mr Douglas,' observed Dee while Justine simply stared, her breath taken away by its sheer beauty.

'Isn't it?' He nodded. 'The only problem is, the Casa Rafael isn't mine. It belongs to friends of friends. But you're quite right, it really is beautiful and the views from the *naya* are breathtaking because you can see down the entire valley.'

'What's a *naya*?' asked Justine.

'The verandah, or terrace,' he explained. 'That's what they call them in this part of Spain. But why don't you come and see for yourselves. Come for lunch tomorrow — pool party, dress casual.'

Justine felt her heart leap at the invitation but before she could reply, Dee said casually, 'Thanks, we just might take you up on that.'

3

Justine slept well only awaking once when it was still dark and hearing the dogs barking in the valley. Then daylight flooded the room and when she opened her eyes, she couldn't think where she was, then she remembered and stretched luxuriously beneath the thin cotton sheet which had been the only covering she had required through the heat of the night.

It seemed cooler and she slipped out of bed and padded across to the window throwing it open and taking in great lungfuls of the sweet morning air. Even as it dawned on her how quiet it seemed the cicadas started up their relentless singing. From her window she could see a corner of the villa next door and she wondered if Cal was awake. She imagined he would be, surely in this climate it would be necessary to do one's stint of writing before the sun got too hot.

Thinking of Cal gave her a warm glow and she thought how nice it was to have him next door. Then she sighed and turned from the window and went into the kitchen to make some tea, no doubt it would be the same old story and Cal would only be interested in Dee, in fact the only boyfriend she'd had who hadn't been interested in Dee had been Gary and that was probably because he'd only met her glamorous friend on a couple of occasions.

She'd loved Gary but when he had gone to London to work their relationship had fizzled out and she later learnt that he was going out with a Swedish girl. In fact she hadn't met anyone since who had really appealed . . . until Cal Douglas had sauntered into her life and stirred something deep inside that she was beginning to think had died. The only problem was that he seemed more interested in Dee than he was in her but maybe this time, things would be different, she thought as she waited for the water to boil, this time Dee wouldn't be interested because for once Dee seemed besotted with someone else.

Justine decided the best thing she could do instead of discouraging Dee in her quest for her Spanish lover was to help her find him. She poured the tea into pottery mugs then carried them through to the other bedroom where she found Dee still asleep in a tangle of sheets. She eventually succeeded in rousing her friend who complained bitterly at the earliness of the hour.

'For goodness sake, Jus, couldn't you sleep?' she mumbled after she'd glared at the clock then buried her head in the pillow again. 'And as for that wretched din outside, don't those blasted crickets ever stop?'

Justine was about to explain that the cicadas had in fact only just started up but she thought better of it and sat on the edge of the bed and sipped her tea instead.

After a while Dee surfaced enough to drink her tea and Justine wondered how she managed to look good first thing in the morning before she'd barely had time to open her eyes.

'Shall we have breakfast outside on the verandah?' she asked Dee after a while.

'Don't you mean the *naya*?' she grunted.

'Oh, yes, the *naya*.' Justine smiled. 'If you like, if it's warm enough. Alfresco living is great while it's warm but as soon as the conditions waver it's murder as far as I'm concerned. Some of the barbecues we have at home or on the boat end up to be horrendous in the teeth of a force ten.'

'Cal was asking about your boat,' said Justine.

'Was he? What did he say?' Dee frowned.

'He only asked who you crewed for then he asked me if I'd done any sailing.'

'You didn't tell him about Ramon?'

46

Justine shook her head. 'No, I didn't.'

'Good. I don't want him to know.'

'Why?'

She shrugged then swung her legs over the side of the bed. 'I don't know. I suppose I would feel silly. After all even you thought it sounded like the old cliché holiday romance. God knows what Cal Douglas would make of it.'

'Hm . . . true, but have you thought, Dee he might be able to help you find Ramon.'

'How?' Dee had reached the doorway but she paused and looked back, a doubtful frown on her face.

'Think about it, if he's been here doing research he has probably got to know lots of local people — he might have come across your friend.'

Dee wrinkled her nose. 'Hm . . . maybe, but no, I don't want to involve him. Not yet anyway. I have one or two avenues I want to explore first, then if I don't get anywhere, I may ask him.'

'Don't you like him?' asked Justine

47

as she followed Dee onto the *naya*.

'Cal Douglas? Yes, I suppose he's all right . . . but . . . '

'But what?'

'I don't know . . . there's something I can't put my finger on.' She leaned back against the iron balcony and grinned at Justine, 'But you obviously like him and it makes a change to see you interested in someone again . . . don't worry, I won't cramp your style.' She turned her head and glanced down towards the pool. 'Come on, I'll race you into the water.'

'But we haven't got our cossies,' Justine began.

'Who needs them?' With a laugh Dee ran down the steps pulling off the tee shirt she wore in bed, and after only a moment's hesitation, Justine, throwing caution to the winds, pausing only to grab their beach towels that they had hung on the balcony to dry, followed her.

The water was cold but after a short while it felt delicious against their bare skin. They swam then splashed around and all the while Justine kept one eye on the villa next door for she half expected Cal to appear. Dee may not care, but she did. All remained quiet however and Justine pictured him pounding away on his typewriter while they had fun.

At last they climbed from the pool and wrapped themselves in the towels before heading for the villa and a shower before breakfast. They carried trays of freshly squeezed orange juice, toast with Spanish marmalade — made from Seville oranges and laced with orange liqueur — and a pot of hot coffee onto the *naya*.

'This is one of the things I like best about being on holiday,' said Justine, 'Not having to rush, especially in the mornings.'

'You could have fooled me,' grunted Dee, 'after the ungodly hour you yanked me out of bed.' Then she grinned. 'No, I know what you mean, it's bliss, not having the boss breathing down your neck.' She yawned and stretched. 'What do you want to do today?'

'We're going to Cal's for lunch.'

'Oh yes.' Dee replied as if she had forgotten.

Justine looked anxious. 'Was there something else you wanted to do?'

'Not particularly. But I thought I'd find a telephone and ring the wine merchants in Valencia where Ramon works.' As she was speaking a sound filled the air growing steadily nearer and both girls raised their heads.

'Sounds like a motorbike,' said Justine. 'One of those little pop pop types that all the kids in town seem to ride.'

It was indeed a small bike and it roared up the hill and turned in at their gate. Justine was surprised to see that the rider was a woman, a few years older than themselves. She wasn't wearing a crash helmet and she looked Spanish, her black hair secured into an untidy knot at the nape of her neck. She was wearing a black dress that clung to her ample figure. She climbed off the bike and looked up at the *naya*.

'*Hola,*' she said and raised one hand in greeting.

They waved back then stood up as she approached the steps.

'I come to see you have all you want? *Si*?' she said in broken English.

'Oh yes, thank you,' they answered simultaneously then Dee frowned.

'Are you a friend of the Galloways?'

'I Josephina, they not tell you I come?'

By this time she had climbed the steps and was standing before them. Dee suddenly smiled. 'Of course,' she said. 'Josephina, I remember now, Mrs Galloway said if there was anything we wanted we had to contact you.'

'I look after villa when empty,' she explained and my husband, Francisco, he come later and see to the pool. *Si*? Now I clean for you.'

'Oh, I don't think that's necessary,'

muttered Dee. 'We've only been here five minutes.'

Nothing however would put Josephina off. She pitched in and stripped the beds, threw open the windows and washed the tiled floors, then while they were drying she tidied the kitchen returning to polish the tiles with a large soft mop. The girls finished their coffee then as Justine carried the tray to the kitchen Dee followed her and hovered in the doorway. The Spanish woman looked up inquiringly as if she found Dee's presence a hindrance.

'Do you live in Javea?' Justine heard Dee ask at last.

'*Si*, I live there. I always live there,' said Josephina ringing out her dishcloth.

Dee had picked up her handbag which had been lying on the top of the fridge, she began rummaging about inside then produced a photograph which she handed to Josephina.

'Do you know this man?' she asked.

Josephina screwed up her dark eyes as

she stared at it and Justine found herself holding her breath while wanting to see the photo herself. She hadn't thought to ask Dee if she'd had a picture of Ramon.

Slowly Josephina shook her head. 'No . . . I not know him . . . but . . . ' she hesitated and Dee looked eager then she shook her head again. 'No,' she said and handed the photograph back. 'He live in Javea?' she said.

'I'm not sure,' replied Dee. 'But there's a chance he might, are you sure you didn't recognise him? I thought for a moment there . . . '

'No, I not know him, but my cousin, he know everyone.'

'Your cousin?' Hope flared in Dee's blue eyes and Justine craned forward to see the photograph.

'*Si*, my cousin, Carlos he work in market. Leather stall, ask for Carlos, say Josephina send you and show him picture. He know,' she said then glancing again at the photograph she said, 'he . . . handsome.' Then she laughed, flashed her dark eyes suggestively, shrugged and turned back to her cleaning.

Ramon Amador was indeed handsome as Justine saw for herself when Dee handed her the picture and the two girls wandered back onto the *naya*.

'You didn't say you had this,' she said and there was an accusing note in her voice.

'You didn't ask,' replied Dee shortly. 'Ramon didn't know I had it either,' she said as an afterthought. 'He hates having his photograph taken but I managed to snap him unawares.'

'It's obviously taken at Cowes,' observed Justine as she studied the profile of the handsome Spaniard. He was in evening dress standing at the rail of a yacht while behind him could be seen the flags and masts of the Royal Yacht *Britannia*.

'Yes,' Dee sighed as if it had all happened a long time ago instead of only two months before. 'It was the night of the ball at the Royal

Corinthian. Ramon didn't have evening dress with him so we had to hire the suit. It was a fabulous evening, we danced until four then after the champagne breakfast we . . . ' she trailed off and looked away.

'Yes?' prompted Justine after a while. 'What happened then.'

Dee frowned and shook her head.

'Can't you tell me about it?' asked Justine gently.

'You'll think I'm dreadful, when that picture was taken I'd only known him two days . . . '

'And . . . ?'

'I slept with him for the first time that night.' Dee looked up sharply and her eyes were suddenly bright. 'I know you won't approve, Jus, but I couldn't help myself. From the moment I set eyes on him I wanted him. I'd never believed in love at first sight, but this was different. It was as if I was under his spell and would do anything he wanted.'

'Oh Dee . . . ' Justine stared at her.

Then softly she said, 'That's not like you. You usually play hard to get.'

'I know.' Dee pulled a face. 'I guess I learnt my lesson this time. The trouble was it was all so easy.'

'What do you mean?' Justine frowned but at that moment Josephina appeared on the *naya*.

'I finish now. I come tomorrow. *Adios*.' With a wave of her hand she was gone and moments later they heard the motorbike start up before it roared away down the hill.

When it was silent again save for the singing of the cicadas Justine said, 'Why was it so easy, Dee?'

Her friend shrugged. 'Well, he didn't appear to have any ties and we didn't even have to worry about anywhere to go.'

'Why?'

'I told you, I was looking after the boat for my uncle.'

'But what about the rest of the crew?'

'They'd rented a house in Cowes so

after the day's sailing they went back there leaving me alone on the boat.'

'Only you weren't alone.'

'Only I wasn't alone,' she repeated cryptically. 'Oh why can't I accept it as one of those things, a beautiful affair that has no future? They happen, after all. But I was convinced there was more to it than that and I thought he felt so too.'

'Do you think he was married, Dee?' She said it gently but it was time it was voiced.

Dee however seemed to have given that aspect some considerable thought. 'No, I don't think he was.'

'But did you actually ask him?'

'Not exactly, no,' she admitted.

'And what if he had said he was married, would it have made any difference?'

'I don't think it would. I know that sounds awful but I was simply head over heels and I don't think any force on earth would have stopped us.'

They were silent for a long while,

Dee obviously lost in her memories. Two golden lizards were playing in the sunlight on the steps darting in and out of the stonework then hiding beneath clumps of brightly coloured mesembryanthemums and although the girls watched them their thoughts were elsewhere. It was Dee who broke the silence. 'Do you understand now why I need to find him?'

Justine nodded slowly. 'Yes, I believe I do. Maybe this Carlos will recognise him,' she added optimistically.

Dee nodded. 'I hope so and I'll phone the wine company in Valencia and see if they can give me any clues.'

There had been no sign of Cal that morning and Justine had pictured him hard at work but that theory was exploded at around eleven thirty when they heard the sound of a car coming up the hill. Moments later Cal's Renault pulled into his drive and they heard him slam the door then his face appeared over the wall.

'Hi there, girls. Just got up?'

'We've been up hours!' exclaimed Justine indignantly aware that her heart had begun to beat very fast. 'You were so quiet we thought you must be working.'

'I have been working,' he said briefly then added, 'and shopping. It isn't every day I have two lovely ladies coming for lunch.' He glanced at his watch. 'Why don't you come on over and try out my pool.'

Dee flung down the paperback she had been reading and stood up. 'I was beginning to feel idle, come on Jus, I suppose we'd better wear cossies this time.' She gave a wicked grin.

'Don't bother on my account,' called Cal over his shoulder as he disappeared from their view.

Fifteen minutes later the girls strolled round to the Casa Rafael. Justine was wearing a floral patterned sundress over her bikini and Dee had pulled on a pair of khaki shorts and a halter necked sun top. In her canvas beach bag Justine had packed towels and the suncream which she knew Dee would be needing before long.

They rounded the corner of the villa and the sheer beauty of the place instantly engulfed them. It was two storeys high and a spiral staircase wound itself round the outside of the building. On the ground floor a large *naya* of blue and white mosaic tiles beneath high cool archways was strewn with padded sunbeds. Two low tables with ceramic tops in ancient Spanish designs held glasses and bowls of black olives. The *naya* faced a large swimming pool surrounded by tubs of bright flowering shrubs, and beyond a garden fringed with palms and olive and fig trees.

They were still staring when Cal appeared at the top of the spiral staircase. He was wearing a black tee shirt and blue jeans cut off at the thighs so that the edges were ragged against his skin. Justine felt her pulse race as his gaze flickered over them both, then for a brief delicious moment came back to rest on her. Then the moment was gone as Dee said, 'Oh there you are, we were just admiring all this opulence. Shall we come up?'

'Yes, come on. I'll show you round before we have a swim.'

It was obvious from the antique oak furniture, and the amount of personal possessions that the villa was a permanent residence and not just a holiday home. The lounge on the first floor which opened onto a second naya was quietly elegant in shades of beige and old rose while hand woven Spanish rugs covered the highly polished marbled floors and lighted cabinets housed collections of finest porcelain and cut glass.

'I like this,' said Dee striding out onto the *naya*.

Justine turned, suddenly very aware of Cal beside her and for one brief moment they were alone. Their eyes met and she saw the unmistakable admiration in his as he allowed his gaze yet again to wander over her.

Then Dee called from outside. 'I say, Justine come and have a look at this view,' and Justine, with a quick smile at Cal reluctantly went to join her.

The view took in the whole of the valley, the bluey-green of the terraced hills opposite and the faint misty purple of the far mountains. For several moments the two girls just stood and drank in the magnificence of the scene.

'Who did you say this place belongs to?' asked Dee at last.

'Friends of friends,' replied Cal.

'I know, but who are they exactly, are they British?' She turned as she spoke and looked back into the villa.

'I believe they are,' said Cal vaguely then he added, 'I think they've been here for about five years. Apparently he's a lawyer.'

'So where are they at the moment?'

He appeared to hesitate then said, 'In Australia on holiday,' then swiftly changing the subject, 'Can I get you girls a drink?'

While he was in the kitchen Justine found herself wondering where Cal worked. There was no sign of a desk or a typewriter and she wondered if he wrote everything in longhand. Later as they relaxed on the sunbeds sipping chilled wine she asked him.

'I didn't want to mess up the house with my rubbish so I keep it confined to my bedroom.'

'Do you type up your notes?' she asked.

'Yes, I have a portable typewriter,' he replied. Then setting down his empty glass he stood up and peeled off his tee shirt. 'There's time for a swim before lunch.'

The girls agreed and within minutes they were splashing around in the pool. Cal was obviously a strong swimmer and after a while he and Dee began counting laps while Justine was content to relax on a lilo. In the end Dee had to admit defeat and laughing and gasping she trod water while Cal continued to streak up and down the pool with a strong overarm stroke. Then even he had had enough and they climbed out of the water letting the hot sun dry their bodies before moving into the shade of the *naya* for lunch. It was while they were eating crusty rolls, olives, cheese and gherkins and drinking more sparkling wine that Dee brought the conversation back to Cal's work.

'Has your book been commissioned?' she said.

'Uh, no,' he replied his mouth full of bread.

'Isn't that frightfully risky?' asked Dee. Then glancing down at her arms she said, 'Oh my God, I'm burning again.' She moved her chair into the shade. 'What was I saying? Oh yes, your book. I don't know much about publishing but I understood that one usually gets someone to commission that type of book before completing it.'

His reply was casual. 'I have every faith in my agent. He liked the original idea and doesn't think he'll have any problem selling the book.'

'Have you written others?' asked Justine.

'This is the first of this type, the others have been more of the text book variety.'

'So you're really a technical author?'

He nodded then stood up. 'You could say that. Now, who would like more wine?'

He refilled their glasses then his own then he sat down again. 'So have you girls made any plans about what you want to do or where you want to go?' As he spoke he picked up a newspaper from the floor. 'Here's a local rag if you're interested.' He passed it to Justine who was relieved to see it was in English.

'We want to go to the market tomorrow,' said Dee.

'I'll run you down there,' he said, 'then if you like, I could pick you up later.'

'I say, this looks fun,' said Justine suddenly looking up from the newspaper.

'There are fiestas on this week.'

'There are a lot of those,' remarked Cal. 'The Spanish love them.'

'There are to be parades commemorating the battles between Moors and the Christians,' added Justine excitedly.

'They're quite spectacular I believe.'

'Have you seen one?' asked Dee and Cal shook his head.

'No I haven't. Maybe we should all go. Would you like to?'

'Oh yes,' replied Justine knowing that this was something she would enjoy, but equally with a growing certainty she was coming to realise she would enjoy any arrangement that included Cal.

4

They dozed after lunch although Justine found it difficult to sleep because she was so aware of Cal. His long lightly tanned limbs were totally relaxed and she took the opportunity to study his features unobserved. The fascinating golden eyes were closed now, the lids hooded while the strong jawline with its slightly cleft chin was resting on his chest. The tawny coloured hair streaked back from its widow's peak above brooding brows while the line of his nose was definitely hawk-like.

She stirred restlessly suddenly filled with a strange desire for the man at her side and she imagined him making love to her. So wild and improbable did her imaginings become that when they were all awoken by the ringing of a telephone she was overcome with hot confusion as if the other two had read her thoughts.

Cal groaned, passed a hand across his face then struggled to his feet. With a muttered apology he disappeared inside the villa. The girls were silent for a while then Dee gave a loud sigh. 'You know something, Jus? I could get used to this way of life,' she said then sitting forward she eased her lounger into the sun. 'Did you bring that suncream with you?' she asked.

Justine smiled, rummaged in her bag then threw the plastic tube of cream at Dee.

'Thanks.' Slowly Dee began rubbing the cream into her arms.

'Here let me help you with that.'

Justine glanced up sharply and saw that Cal had come silently back onto the *naya* and was watching Dee. She smiled provocatively up at him then held out the tube. Justine felt her heart lurch uncomfortably as he crouched beside Dee, squeezed some cream onto the palm of his hand then began rubbing it into her shoulders and back. When he reached the strap of her bikini she unfastened it at the same time managing to hold the front over her breasts.

He laughed. 'Can't have any white areas, can we?'

Justine swallowed and looked away. She wished she could be that uninhibited but she knew she would have been covered in confusion especially after the erotic thoughts she had just been having.

As if he knew what she was thinking he turned to her. 'What about you, Justine? I'd better extend the same service to you both.'

'Oh Justine's all right,' grumbled Dee, 'she never burns, she just tans deeper and deeper. It makes me sick.'

He smiled, his eyes meeting Justine's and her heart lurched again crazily. 'She's right,' he agreed. 'You really are the most gorgeous colour and with your dark hair it makes you look quite exotic, a bit like one of the locals.'

'You haven't got very brown,' remarked Dee can-didly. 'How long did you say you've been here?'

'I'll have you know I've been working, not loafing around in the sun.'

Suddenly Dee stood up and fastening her bikini she bent down and took a notepad from the pocket of her shorts which were lying on the ground. 'Do you think I could use your telephone, Cal?' she asked casually. Then seeing his surprise, she added, 'Don't worry, it's a local call, I don't want to phone home.'

He only hesitated fractionally then said, 'Of course, the phone's upstairs in the lounge, help yourself.' He watched as Dee climbed the spiral staircase then as she reached the top he called, 'Will you want a directory?'

'No thanks,' she called over the banister rail, 'I have the number.'

Justine guessed she must be going to phone the wine merchants in Valencia but she was unprepared when Cal said, 'I didn't realise you knew anyone locally.'

'I don't,' admitted Justine. 'But Dee's been to Spain before. Maybe she got friendly with someone then.' Much as she liked the idea of being alone with Cal, Justine wished her friend wouldn't get her into such awkward situations. If she didn't want Cal to know about Ramon, fine, but she shouldn't put her, Justine in the position of having to lie for her.

As the minutes ticked by she became more and more anxious especially as Cal threw several glances in the direction of the villa. At last in an attempt to ease the tension Justine said, 'Do you know very much about Victorian history, Cal?'

'Hardly anything I'm afraid,' he admitted. 'My period is European medieval history.'

'Did you read history at university?' she asked.

'Uh, yes.'

'Oh, which one did you go to?

I didn't go to university and I've regretted it ever since. Money was tight in those days my mother couldn't afford to let me go.'

'Is your father dead?'

She nodded. 'Yes, he died when I was a child.'

'I take it money isn't a problem for your friend?' he asked casually.

She gave a rueful smile. 'Dee's family have always been well off.'

'What does her father do?'

'He's managing director of an aircraft company.'

'On the Isle of Wight?'

'Yes, as I told you, the family home is in Bembridge but they have a flat in London as well and of course they entertain a lot.'

'I expect she has lots of friends.'

'Lots,' admitted Justine wondering how they had managed to start talking about Dee again.

'Does she have a steady boyfriend?' he asked quietly.

Justine felt a pang of misery. He

could only want to know that for one reason. She was saved from answering by the sudden appearance of Dee on the spiral staircase.

She looked up anxiously and saw that Dee's expression was set. It didn't look as if she'd had much luck with her phone call. As she flopped down onto her sunbed again Cal said, 'Did you get through all right?'

'Oh, yes, yes thanks.' Her reply was abrupt then she fell into a moody silence.

Justine was beginning to feel uncomfortable when Cal stood up and said, 'Who would like some iced tea?'

'Yes please,' said Justine glad of the diversion. 'That sounds lovely.'

Dee however stood up. 'Not for me thanks,' she said. 'I'm going back to wash my hair.' With that she picked up her shorts and top and with a curt nod to Cal and brief thanks for the lunch, she marched off leaving Justine to apologise for her rudeness.

'It's OK,' said Cal. 'It's probably the

heat, it gets to people. Not to worry, I'll go and get the iced tea for us.'

He disappeared indoors leaving Justine thinking that it was more likely to have been the phone call that had upset Dee rather than the heat.

Cal seemed to be gone for a long time, but at last he appeared with two tall glasses of iced tea complete with slices of lemon. It tasted delicious and Justine lay back happily, content to have Cal to herself with no competition from Dee.

He however seemed on edge and while he was drinking his tea he more than once glanced in the direction of the villa next door. Justine came to the miserable conclusion that it was only Dee he was interested in and that she didn't stand a chance.

'So do you have lots of friends and do a lot of entertaining as well?' he asked suddenly as he set his glass down on the tiles beside him.

'Good heavens, no. That isn't my scene at all.'

74

He stared at her thoughtfully, 'That's strange, with you two being such good friends, I would have thought your interests would have been similar.'

'It was horse riding that brought us together,' explained Justine thinking how handsome he looked with the bright sunlight shining on his hair. 'It's a love we still share, when we get the opportunity. Other than that, Dee's lifestyle is very different from mine.'

'Yet you seem to get on well.'

She shrugged. 'I suppose it's a case of opposites attracting.'

'So don't you see each other socially at all?' he persisted.

'Occasionally, the odd dinner or party, usually at Dee's home.'

'And the sailing,' he said.

'The sailing?' she looked up and frowned.

'Yes, you said you'd been sailing with Dee and her family.'

'Oh that was ages ago.'

'So you weren't involved with this year's Admiral's Cup?'

'Heavens no, that was Dee, they wouldn't let me anywhere near a boat for that.' She pulled a face and Cal laughed.

'I believe they have lots of parties during Cowes week?' he asked casually.

She laughed. 'Oh yes, it's a tremendous atmosphere, they have open-air bars on all the marinas, the pubs stay open all day and the dances go on all night.'

'Really?' He looked fascinated. 'Did you go to any?'

'I have in the past but not this year. Dee went to the Royal Corinthian Ball — members of the Royal Family usually attend that.'

'And you missed out?'

'Yes, I have to make do with the ghosts of Victoria and Albert at Osborne House.' She laughed again thinking how easy it was to talk to him.

He too laughed, then said, 'And who did Dee have as her escort for that?'

Without thinking she said, 'Oh she

went with Ramon.'

He raised his eyebrows. 'Ramon?'

She felt herself grow hot as she realised her mistake. 'Oh it was just someone she'd met that week, I don't know him.'

'Ramon — sounds Spanish,' he mused.

'Er, I wouldn't know,' she replied quickly then in an effort to change the subject and wishing that Dee wouldn't be so silly about not letting Cal know about Ramon, she said, 'You'll have to visit the island sometime and see all these things for yourself. The islanders are very hospitable, we'll give you a warm welcome.'

'Can I take that to mean you have no-one special in your life?'

He was staring at her intently and there was something about the look in his eyes that made her heart beat even faster. 'Yes,' she replied softly. 'You can take it to mean just that, there isn't anyone special in my life — now.'

'You mean there was?'

'Yes,' she admitted, 'there was.'

'And who was he?'

She smiled and looked embarrassed. 'A boy who came to live next door, we went out together for some time then . . . then he went to London to work . . . ' she shrugged. 'The last I heard he was dating a Swedish girl.'

'And how long ago was that?'

'Oh some time now,' she admitted trying to sound casual, not wanting him to think she was totally inexperienced.

'And there hasn't been anyone since?'

'Not really — at least no-one serious.' She glanced at him then summoning the courage from somewhere she said, 'And what about you? Is there anyone special in your life?' She held her breath as she waited for his reply, dreading what she might be about to hear, knowing that it mattered terribly that he should be unattached.

He was silent then he said slowly, 'Like you, there was someone once . . . she was special, very special. We

78

lived together for a time but . . .'
he shrugged and spread his hands, 'it
didn't work out.'

'What went wrong?'

'I don't know, my lifestyle didn't
help, the hours I kept were erratic, she
couldn't stand it.'

Justine nodded understandingly.
'Burning the midnight oil,' she said.

'Sorry?' He glanced at her vaguely.

'Isn't that what writers do?' she
asked, 'burn the midnight oil?'

'Oh, yes,' he said quickly. 'Yes, that
was a problem, whenever she wanted
to do something I had a deadline to
meet. In the end it all got too much
and we split.' He sighed and narrowing
his eyes against the sun he stared into
the distance, at the bluish terraces on
the far hillsides and the dark columns
of tall poplars. He seemed pensive and
Justine was reluctant to intrude sensing
his memories were precious and that
this woman, whoever she was had
indeed been very special. He'd said
they'd lived together and the thought

of him making love to some unknown woman gave her a sudden sharp thrill of pain. She stirred restlessly. Whatever was the matter with her? The heat must have got to her, never mind Dee, for she could never remember having such erotic thoughts about anyone before, let alone someone she'd only just met. The sight and close proximity of his nearly naked body didn't help and she was just on the point of saying that she really ought to go when he suddenly sat upright and said, 'How about another swim?'

Standing up he reached out his hand and before she had time to think she had held out her own hand and he had grasped it. His touch, strong and dry sent shivers down her spine in spite of the heat and as he pulled her to her feet she found his eyes gazing into hers. Then he was leading her towards the pool, turning so that he took both her hands in his before lowering himself into the water.

Gingerly she followed taking one step

at a time as the cool water crept up their bodies and all the time her gaze never left his. Before she knew what was happening he had let go of her hands placing his own on her shoulders and gently pushing downwards so that the water covered her until briefly they were totally submerged and when she surfaced, gasping and laughing, she couldn't see him for the water in her eyes. She felt his hands either side of her face and for one exquisite moment his lips covered hers. The kiss was warm, tender and she wanted it to last forever but then he was gone, slicing through the water away from her, leaving her wondering if she'd imagined it.

They swam for about half an hour enjoying the sun, the water and each other's company and too soon it came to an end, Cal climbed from the pool and vigorously towelled himself. Justine watched him then she too reluctantly climbed from the water and wrapped herself in one of the large brightly patterned beach towels.

'Would you like something else to drink?' Cal asked over his shoulder as he padded towards the *naya*.

'No thank you, I really should be getting back. Dee will be wondering where I've got to.'

He turned and waited for her and as she caught him up, he smiled and she felt as if her legs had turned to water.

'Thank you for lunch and the swim,' she added aware of the look of amusement that had entered his eyes.

'You must come again,' he said.

'No, it's our turn next. You must come and have a meal with us.'

'Thanks, I should like that. It gets lonely eating by myself. Now, if you're going to the market tomorrow, may I suggest an early start. It gets crowded down there. Supposing I pick you up about eight thirty?'

She was about to ask if he could make it later when she changed her mind. After all, it was for Dee's benefit that they were going so she would just have to get up early.

She was in the same defiant mood when she confronted Dee ten minutes later. Dee had washed her hair and was lying in the sun drying it.

'Did you have to be so rude?' Justine stared down at her friend.

Dee looked up, shielding her eyes from the sun with her hand. 'What are you talking about?'

'To Cal, after the lunch he made us and everything, you could at least have been civil. And to think he let you use his phone . . . and you didn't even offer to pay!'

'Have you quite finished?' There was an amused expression on Dee's face as she stared up at Justine. 'As it happens I did thank him for lunch . . . and I didn't offer to pay for the call because, well, one doesn't . . . and if by not being civil you're referring to the fact that I went off and left you, well all I can say to that is that you're being damned ungrateful.'

'What do you mean?' Justine demanded.

'I thought I was doing you a favour, it's obvious you fancy him like hell so I thought I'd leave you to it for a while. And if what I saw going on in the pool just now was anything to go by, I'd say it was a good job I did.'

Justine was shocked into embarrassed silence and she began kicking the wicker leg on one of the sunbeds with the toe of her espradrille, then looking up she caught the wicked glint of laughter in Dee's eyes. 'You really are impossible, Dee you know how shy I get over these things. I'm not like you, I wish I were, but I'm not.'

'You mean like sleeping with someone on the first date?' asked Dee caustically.

'I didn't mean that,' said Justine quickly then peering closely at her friend she said, 'Did you find out anything? The phone call . . . ? Did you get through to the wine merchants?'

'Oh yes, I got through. I spoke to a

very charming man whose English was really rather good.'

'And . . . ? Did you ask about Ramon?'

'Oh yes, I asked. He'd never heard of him.'

'Oh, Dee.'

'He said no one of that name had ever worked for the company. I also asked if they'd been involved in any sponsorship for Cowes week.'

'I suppose he'd never heard of Cowes either.'

'Believe it or not but that part was true. Apparently the UK branch of the company was involved with sponsorship for the Admiral's Cup. But he'd never heard of Ramon.'

'Dee, I don't know what to say,' said Justine.

'How about, 'I told you so'?'

'I wouldn't say that . . . ever.'

Dee stared at her then quietly she said, 'No Jus, you wouldn't, would you?'

'I think,' said Justine slowly, 'that

I'm beginning to understand how you feel about him.'

'So I'm right then, about you and Mr Next Door? You are smitten by him?'

'Yes, I suppose I am,' said Justine glancing over her shoulder at the bougainvillaea covered wall that separated them from the Casa Rafael. 'I don't know what's wrong with me, it isn't like me at all to fall for someone as quickly as that. It usually takes me ages just to get to know someone.'

'Ah, that's what happens when it's the real thing,' said Dee. 'It jumps up and grabs you by the throat.' She narrowed her eyes speculatively. 'And how about him, does he feel the same way about you?'

'I've no idea,' protested Justine.

'He seemed pretty interested just now,' Dee jerked her head in the direction of the next door pool and Justine felt herself grow hot at the memory and she gave a nervous laugh then she said, 'If I'm truthful, I think he's more interested in you than in me.'

'Rubbish,' said Dee and stood up tossing her golden head and running her fingers through her hair. 'I'm not his type and he knows it, neither is he mine.' She began to walk towards the villa then as she reached the steps she paused and with a brief backward glance she said, 'Trouble is, I'm not completely sure he's your type either. There's something about our new friend, Jus, that I don't trust and I don't want you to get hurt.'

5

Justine had followed Dee but at her words she stared at her in dismay. 'You really don't like Cal, do you? Not just because he isn't your type, there's something else isn't there?'

Dee shrugged then carried on up the steps. 'I don't know what it is, Justine, but like I said, I'm sure I've seen him somewhere before. If only I could remember where, perhaps I would know why he makes me nervous.'

'Well, it couldn't have been on the island, so it was probably on one of your trips to London.'

'I know,' replied Dee thoughtfully, 'but that's what doesn't quite fit. Never mind, maybe it will come to me. In the meantime just take things easy,' she said then catching sight of her friend's expression she pulled a face, 'I know that sounds good coming from me, but

I don't want to see you get hurt.'

They'd changed the subject then and prepared a salad for their evening meal then afterwards they'd climbed to the top of the hill behind the villa and sat on the rocky ground enjoying the view; the deep valley with the mountains behind, the town with the port in the distance and beyond, the vast glittering expanse of the Mediterranean. They watched the sun go down, the sky becoming a furnace of glowing orange streaked with shades of pink eventually softening into twilight then as the darkness crept up on them they watched the circulating rays of light from a lighthouse on a pinnacle of rock overlooking the port.

'What will you do next, about Ramon?' asked Justine at last.

'Now I've had time to think I've decided I'll show his photograph to Josephina's cousin, Carlos and see if he knows him.'

'And if he doesn't?'

'I don't know.'

They were silent again and a little breeze sprung up around them disturbing the scent of the pines and rustling the coarse grass that grew in great tufts between the boulders.

'I do wish you'd tell Cal,' said Justine at last. 'I'm sure he'd be only too willing to help.'

Dee didn't answer immediately then she sighed. 'I suppose you're right. I guess I was being silly. I tell you what, if I don't get anywhere with Carlos, I'll tell Cal and we'll see if he can suggest anything.'

'That's better,' said Justine and there was a note of relief in her voice. She hadn't told Dee that she had inadvertently mentioned Ramon's name to Cal.

'Talking of the market,' she said as they began the walk down the steep hillside, 'Cal said we would need to go early because it gets crowded. He said he'd pick us up at half past eight.' She threw Dee an anxious glance. 'I didn't think you'd be very happy about that.'

Dee gave a short laugh. 'I can get up early when I want to.'

All was quiet when they reached the villa but as they walked up the drive Justine suddenly had the impression that someone was watching them. She glanced over her shoulder but the road was empty and the next door villa in darkness.

She wondered if Cal was out, if he'd gone to bed, or if he was simply sitting in the darkness. Was it him who was watching them return? She felt her spine tingle and knew it wasn't fear but excitement at the thought that he may be watching for her to return.

Justine slept well and awoke to the delicious aroma of sizzling bacon. For a puzzled moment she lay still then slipping out of bed she padded out of the room.

In the kitchen she found Dee in front of the cooker. A jug of freshly squeezed orange juice stood on the fridge, coffee bubbled in the percolator and even as she stared in amazement two slices of golden brown toast popped up from the toaster.

'You look as if you've seen a ghost.' Dee laughed as she served the bacon on to plates which she put in the oven to keep warm then broke two eggs into the frying pan. 'I can cook you know.'

'So I see,' observed Justine. 'But I was more concerned about your figure.'

'What's wrong with my figure?' demanded Dee.

'Nothing from where I'm standing,' said a voice from the doorway.

Both girls spun round and found Cal lounging in the open doorway. 'I'm sorry,' he said helplessly. 'It was the smell, it wafted across the garden and I had to come and see if my imagination was playing a cruel trick.'

'It wasn't your imagination,' said Dee. 'Go and find yourself a seat on the *naya*,' she added as she took more bacon from the fridge. 'You too,' she said to Justine. 'Make the most of this spell of domesticity because it may not last.'

'I thought I was imagining things too,' said Justine as she followed Cal out onto the *naya*. 'In England Dee wouldn't even look at fried food, let alone cook it. She always says it's far too fattening.'

'We all do things on holiday we wouldn't normally think of,' he said and his eyes met hers.

Her heart had been doing strange things since he had appeared and she wondered if he was referring to that kiss in the pool the day before.

They fell silent for a moment, the only sounds the singing of the cicadas and Dee clattering around in the kitchen.

'Cal,' Justine said uncertainly.

'Yes,' he looked up with his heart-stopping smile and she almost chickened out. Then glancing into the villa to reassure herself that Dee was still occupied, she said, 'Do you remember when we were talking about Cowes week and you asked me who went to the Royal Corinthian Ball with Dee?'

He nodded. 'Yes and you said some Spanish name, Raoul? No, Ramon, that was it.'

'Yes,' said Justine quickly with another furtive glance into the villa. 'Well, if Dee tells you anything about Ramon don't let on that I mentioned him.'

He chuckled. 'Let the cat out of the bag, did you?'

'Not exactly, but I wasn't supposed to say anything.'

'Who is he?' Cal looked amused. 'A secret married lover?'

'I don't know.' She shrugged helplessly then as Dee began to walk through the lounge with plates of breakfast she frowned and muttered, 'Please?'

He leaned forward and touching the side of his nose in a conspiratorial gesture, he said, 'Mum's the word.'

She smiled gratefully, then her attention was taken by Dee who was complaining that the plates were very hot and that she had to put them down.

They had finished breakfast, cleared away and were in Cal's Renault by exactly eight thirty.

'I'll bet you never thought we'd make it,' said Dee triumphantly as they sped down the hill.

'I had my doubts,' he said with a laugh.

'It's very good of you to take us,' said Justine.

'I have a few things to collect, then it's back to the grindstone.' He pulled a face.

'Aren't you staying with us?' said Justine trying not to let her disappointment show.

'Afraid not. I've reached a crucial stage and I'll be hard at it all day. But I'll come down later and pick you up.'

'That's kind of you but if you're too busy . . .'

'No, that's OK. By late afternoon I will have had enough and I'll be glad of a break. Maybe we could have something to eat in one of the beachside restaurants, the local fish dishes are out of this world.'

'That sounds a marvellous idea,' said Dee then pointing as a small motor bike roared past them through the orange groves she said, 'There's Josephina, she'll never believe we are up and out at this time of the morning.'

'Who's Josephina?' asked Cal.

'She's the lady who looks after the villa for Mrs Galloway,' explained Justine.

'You must have seen her,' said Dee. 'She goes up every day.' Cal didn't reply and Dee threw him a glance. 'If you haven't seen her you must have heard her. That bike can be heard for miles around.'

'They are noisy things, aren't they? But they seem to be a way of life here,' he replied smoothly. 'Here we are,' he added moments later as the market came into sight. 'I'll find somewhere to park, I want to buy some fruit.'

Justine was surprised that Cal didn't seem to know Josephina for he had indicated that he'd been at the Casa

Rafael for some while and if that was the case, he couldn't have failed to notice the comings and goings next door. She dismissed the thought however as he parked the car and they scrambled out and walked down the narrow road to the large open air market.

The sun already felt hot on their bare limbs and as they approached the brightly coloured canvas stalls Justine said she wanted to buy a hat to protect her head from the heat.

'You'll be able to get one here,' said Cal. 'The straw and cane work is hand crafted and very attractive but be careful, they like you to barter with them, but they set their prices high to start with.'

They were quickly absorbed into the noisy, colourful throng, surrounded by hundreds of dark-eyed swarthy locals, some shopping, others anxious to sell, especially to unsuspecting pink-skinned tourists.

The wares were varied; from fresh

produce; fruit, vegetables and tired looking cut flowers, to stalls stocked with fish, sweets and confectionery. They moved on through the narrow aisles where they found clothing, hand crafted Moorish jewellery, Spanish fans, leather work, pottery and ceramics and the locally crafted cane work.

Flamenco music blared from one stallholder's transistor and Justine laughed with delight as the atmosphere captured her imagination. They tried on straw hats while the sombre-faced stallholder held a mirror for them to see their reflections, then when they had made their choice Justine became aware that Dee was getting edgy. No doubt she was only waiting for Cal to go before she approached one of the stallholders with her photograph of Ramon.

Almost as if he knew what was going on in their minds Cal suddenly said, 'Well I'm going to leave you girls now. Shall I meet you at the beach about six?'

'That'll be fine,' said Dee as if she couldn't wait for him to be gone.

'Goodbye then, have a good time.' For a moment his eyes met Justine's then with a wave of his hand he was gone.

With a sinking feeling Justine watched him pushing his way through the crowd. It was all very well Dee wanting to get rid of him so that she could pursue Ramon, but Cal Douglas was the only man in her life and she wished desperately he was spending the day with her and not going back to the Casa Rafael to work.

When she could no longer see his mass of tawny hair she sighed and turned away only to find that Dee had already fished the photograph out of her handbag.

'Now comes the difficult bit.' Dee frowned and looked round. There was one stall behind them hung with leather jackets and handbags and another further down the aisle on the opposite side. 'Well here goes, we've got to start somewhere,' she said and strode purposefully towards an elderly, wizened faced Spaniard who, sensing a sale looked up eagerly. His attitude changed when it became apparent that she wasn't interested in his merchandise and he became surly, shaking his head when she showed him the picture then turning away.

'Somehow I don't think that was Carlos,' said Justine. 'In fact I would imagine that Josephina's cousin would be younger than that. Look the men on that stall over there,' she pointed down the aisle, 'look younger and they seem friendlier too.'

The two young Spaniards were indeed friendly, too friendly in fact as Dee asked if either of them were called Carlos. After a great deal of nudging and speculation as the two young men appraised the English girls, Justine pulled Dee away. 'Neither of them are Carlos,' she said laughingly for there had been nothing offensive about them.

They tried two more stalls, the second selling every type of leather belt imaginable and it was at this one that they struck lucky. When Dee asked the stallholder if his name was Carlos he shook his head and pointed to the stall which backed on to his.

Dee dashed down the aisle and as she followed, even Justine felt a growing sense of excitement. By the time she caught her up, Dee was talking to a swarthy Spaniard of around thirty and Justine guessed this was the elusive Carlos. Dee again produced the photograph and thrust it under the man's nose.

'Do you know this man?' she asked breathlessly.

Justine was watching the Spaniard carefully and for the briefest of moments she detected a flash of recognition on his heavy features. Then it was gone and he shrugged and would have handed the picture back to Dee.

'Oh please, look again,' said Dee urgently. 'Josephina said you knew everyone, she said you would be sure to know him.'

At the mention of his cousin's name, Carlos who had turned away, paused and looked at Dee. Then he reached out a grimy hand, took the photograph again and stared at it.

'His name is Ramon,' persisted Dee. 'And I think he lives in this area.'

Carlos was silent then a torrent of Spanish fell from his lips and with a gesture of disgust he thrust the picture back at Dee.

Dee blinked and started at him in dismay. 'Oh, what did you say, don't you speak English?' She turned wildly to Justine who could only shake her head in bewilderment then she appealed to the other stall holder. 'What did he say?' she pleaded, but he too turned away, a surly expression on his face.

Unable to bear the despair on Dee's face, Justine stepped forward. 'Are you sure you can't help us?' she asked Carlos carefully. Somehow she imagined that Carlos' usual expression was cheerful, not the sullen look that was on his face now.

He stared at her, then another stream of Spanish followed but this time she was able to recognise one word. He turned then and stamped off into the dark recess at the back of his stall.

'Oh, please, don't go,' wailed Dee, then she stopped as Justine put a restraining hand on her arm.

'Come on Dee, there's no point. He doesn't want to tell us more.' She dragged her friend away from the stall.

'He knew something,' protested Dee angrily. 'And I'm sure his English was better than he let on. Well, in future Josephina can keep her objectionable relatives to herself.'

'Calm down,' said Justine. 'There's something I want to tell you.'

'What?' Dee demanded.

'I think you're right about Carlos knowing more than he let on. I also think he recognised Ramon but didn't want to admit it. I don't think he would have said anything at all if we hadn't mentioned Josephina's name.'

'What do you mean?'

'Well, he went on to say a lot more, didn't he?'

'Yes,' she replied hotly, 'and all of it in Spanish, a fat lot of good that was.'

By this time they had reached the end of the stalls and found a low wall in the shade of a large date palm. They sat down facing the colourful market scene stretched out before him. The strains of Bizet's *Carmen* drifted across the stalls and Justine took from her bag a bar of marzipan which she had bought from one of the stalls. She unwrapped the paper, broke off a piece and as she handed it to Dee, she said slowly, 'Don't get too excited, Dee, but I think I understood something Carlos said.'

'What?' Dee turned sharply the piece of marzipan half way to her mouth.

'Yes, he said it twice — the word Altea. It's a town, Dee, quite near here I think. I saw it mentioned in Cal's newspaper yesterday.'

'Are you saying he was trying to tell us that Ramon is in this place . . . Altea?'

'I'm not sure. But it's the best thing we have to go on.'

'I'm going to go back and ask him.' Dee stood up but Justine caught hold of her arm.

'I don't think that's a good idea. He obviously was very reluctant to talk about Ramon.'

'But why? Why should he be?' demanded Dee.

'I don't know.' Justine shrugged. 'Maybe they don't like each other.' She fell silent but a doubt niggled at the back of her mind, the same doubt that had been there since Dee had told her of her relationship with the Spaniard.

'What do we do next?' asked Dee at last.

'Plan a trip to Altea?' asked Justine. Dee nodded. 'I suppose that's all I can do, I don't have anything else to go on. And the days are slipping by.' She looked helplessly at Justine.

'I still think we could ask Cal for help,' said Justine.

Dee was silent, then with a trace of reluctance said, 'All right, I suppose we needn't tell him everything, simply that I want to try and trace a friend who I think might live in Altea.'

'Exactly.' Justine stood up, 'Now, I don't know about you, but I'm fed up with markets, let's walk into town.'

6

They spent the next couple of hours wandering in the old town. Justine marvelled at the ancient buildings with their Gothic windows, the glimpses of courtyards behind iron grills where fountains played on mosaic tiles amidst green ferns, and niches in stonework housing effigies of forgotten saints, but Dee quickly became bored. Her interests lay in what the shops had to offer in Spanish fashions, jewellery or shoes but then she tired of even that and suggested moving on to the beach.

They were standing before a coffee shop and Justine hesitated. 'There was one more place I wanted to visit,' she said. 'Up there on the hill, that church, the one with the blue dome.'

Dee groaned. 'All right. But I'll go in here and wait for you. It's getting so hot.'

'I'll come and have a coffee with you first,' said Justine following her into the shop.

They ordered coffee and pastries and while they were enjoying them Dee said, 'I might go on down to the beach while you're visiting your church, it isn't far to walk and you can join me there when you've finished.'

'OK,' Justine grinned then narrowing her eyes, she said, 'Your shoulders are burning, Dee.'

'Damn, and I haven't got the suncream with me.'

'I don't think that would be enough, it looks as if you should cover yourself up today. Tell you what, let's go in the 'Ladies' before we leave and we'll swap tops, at least mine has sleeves.'

When they left the coffee shop both girls were wearing the sunhats they'd bought in the market, Justine having tucked her hair inside hers for coolness. Dee was wearing Justine's white cotton top while Justine wore Dee's bright red halter suntop. They parted outside the shop after arranging where they should meet, Dee heading for the road to the port and the beach and Justine climbing the hill to the church with the blue dome.

The interior of the Roman Catholic church was large, cool and slightly dim after the bright sunlight outside. There was a strong scent of incense and the chancel area and altar were filled with an interesting collection of ecclesiastical treasures. Justine quickly became absorbed, forgetting the time, the heat outside and even where she was. A few other tourists wandered between the great pillars studying tombs and the statues of saints, their voices muted, hushed in the awesome atmosphere. Two Spanish women dressed in black were arranging lilies at the base of the pulpit and as Justine approached they averted their eyes.

She wasn't sure at what point it happened but gradually Justine became aware of some sensation. It was elusive but at the same time vaguely familiar; a feeling she had experienced only recently, then suddenly she knew what it was and where it had happened before. It was the feeling she'd had only the previous evening when she and Dee had returned from their walk; a feeling of being watched.

Slowly she turned her head. Nothing seemed to have changed, the little knots of tourists still drifted to and fro, the ladies still worked around the pulpit, but then she saw him. In the open doorway at the far end of the church a dark figure, silhouetted against the brightness beyond stood watching her.

She blinked, trying to adjust her vision then her heart thudded as she recognised the tawny coloured hair. Her first thought, as the eeriness of being watched swiftly evaporated, was that he had decided to join them earlier than he had said and her heart leapt with joy.

With a smothered exclamation she

started forward down the nave to join him, but before she'd taken even a couple of steps there was a crash behind her that echoed in the stillness. She stopped and turned then saw that one of the Spanish women had dropped a metal flower container and the two of them were twittering together as they retrieved it from under the pews.

When Justine turned back the doorway was empty.

Barely a minute later she burst out into the sunshine the heat hitting her as if she was entering an oven.

There was no sign of Cal.

Wildly she looked around and to the right of the church she saw an archway covered by the inevitable iron grill which stood open a few inches. Without stopping to think she plunged through and ran along a short passage which opened on to a courtyard behind the church. At the top of a short flight of steps she paused, slightly breathless. The bulk of the vast building of the church blotted out the sunlight and almost the entire area was in shadow. There were three people in the courtyard. A middle-aged Spanish couple and an elderly man. They all looked briefly at Justine then carried on with what they were doing.

As soon as she saw that Cal wasn't there she turned to run again, then she stopped and looked curiously back into the courtyard. There was a strange smell which Justine couldn't place, very different from the incense and the cloying scent of the flowers inside the church. In the high walls there were dozens of tiny black grills and beside each one was a metal plaque. Justine peered at the ones nearest and saw that beside each plaque, which bore a name, was an oval photograph behind a piece of perspex and it was then that she realised that this was a cemetery.

Suddenly she shivered, and it had nothing to do with the fact that the sun was hidden from view.

She turned again and ran to the front of the church and out on to the road. From there she could see all the way down into the town. The heat shimmered above the road and an old man pushing a bicycle was laboriously climbing the hill but still there was no sign of Cal.

Puzzled, she slowly began to walk down the hill. There were very few people about now as it was almost siesta time and as the intense heat hit her shoulders again she wished she was wearing her own cool cotton top that she had loaned to Dee.

Once she glanced back at the church. There had been something eerie about the place and she found herself wondering if she had in fact seen Cal, or whether it had just been wishful thinking and that the figure she'd seen in the doorway had been a figment of her imagination.

As she neared the town however she dismissed that notion. She wasn't a fanciful person and she knew almost without doubt that the person she had seen had been Cal. But if that had been so, why had he disappeared? She was certain he had seen her, so if that was the case, why hadn't he joined her or at least stopped and spoken to her?

Maybe Dee had seen him, she thought as a little later she neared the beach. Then on impulse she decided she wouldn't tell Dee what had happened. Dee had already voiced her distrust of Cal, this would only make her more hostile towards him.

As she began walking along the sea wall scanning the beach for her friend she decided the best thing she could do was to get Cal on his own and ask him why he had acted as he had.

She eventually found Dee stretched out beneath a rented parasol on a sunbed.

They spent a lazy afternoon; a dip in the sea followed by a light lunch and a siesta in the shade of the tall date palms that fringed the beach, then the remainder of the time reading the paperbacks they'd bought at the airport.

Once or twice Justine sensed a restlessness in Dee and she guessed she was getting more anxious about tracing Ramon with every hour of their holiday that passed.

But as six o'clock approached Justine found that she too was getting restless and her gaze kept wandering to the road. Even the thought of Cal made her heart beat faster and she was being forced to admit the powerful effect he was having on her.

When he did arrive it was from the opposite direction to which Justine had expected and they found him suddenly standing beside them. Dee gave a little shriek and flung down her book.

'Good grief, you made me jump. What in the world are you doing creeping up on us like that?'

'Sorry.' He grinned and crouched beside them and Justine found her mouth had suddenly gone dry. 'I walked along the beach.'

'Where's your car?' Dee craned her neck trying to spot the Renault on the esplanade behind them.

'I've parked it in the car park,' he said calmly. Then standing up again he asked, 'Have you had a good day?'

'Pretty good.' Dee yawned and struggled to her feet. 'How about you? What sort of a day have you had? You said you had a lot to do.'

Justine found she was holding her breath as she waited for his reply.

'Oh yes,' he replied. 'I did have a lot to do, and I'm glad to say I got it all done.'

'So you've been slaving over a hot typewriter all day?' Dee grinned.

'You could say that,' he replied smoothly. Then changing the subject he went on, 'So are you ready to eat? There's a super fish restaurant further along that is almost on the beach.'

'Sounds good,' remarked Dee. 'Come on Justine. Hey, are you all right?' She paused, looking down at Justine who was still sitting on her sunbed.

'Yes, I'm fine, thanks.' Justine stood up and without looking at Cal she began to pack their belongings into the beach bag.

Cal had been quite right about the restaurant for it was literally on the beach. They chose large pieces of sole from the display of freshly caught fish then while they waited for it to be cooked they were served with a carafe of white wine, a basket of crusty bread together with a garlic dip and a salad sprinkled with olive oil.

As they sipped the delicious chilled wine Justine could not help but notice that Dee was being unusually friendly towards Cal and she guessed what she was leading up to. And it was while they were enjoying their fish that Dee casually looked up and said, 'Cal, have you heard of a place called Altea?'

He nodded as he took a mouthful of wine. 'Yes, it's a little further down the coast, not that far from here . . . why?'

'I was hoping to go there,' replied Dee carefully.

'Any special reason?' Cal asked without looking up.

Justine was watching Dee and she noticed her usually confident friend looked uncomfortable.

'Someone I know lives in Altea, or at least I think they do,' she said with a frown.

Justine glanced at Cal and saw that he had become very still, his knife and fork poised, then carefully he put them down and looked at Dee.

'Someone you know?' he asked.

Dee shrugged trying to look nonchalant. 'Yes, someone I met back home. I thought it would be nice to look them up.'

'Do you have an address?' asked Cal leaning back in his chair.

'No.' Then seeing Cal's doubtful expression she added, 'I know it's a long shot, but I thought it was worth a try especially as we're so close. In fact,' she hesitated then went on in a rush, 'I was wondering if you would help me to find him.'

'Oh, so it's a he, is it?' Cal smiled.

'Yes, it's a he,' admitted Dee.

In the silence that followed Justine held her breath then Cal said, 'I take it you at least know his name?'

Dee nodded then with a trace of reluctance she said, 'Of course I do, it's Ramon Amador.'

Justine glanced at Cal but not by so much as the flicker of an eyelid did he give away that he had heard that name before. Suddenly she felt a rush of gratitude almost as if they were fellow conspirators, then with a pang she remembered the incident in the church and the fact that he hadn't mentioned it. She wondered whether he could have been simply doing further research and when he had said he'd been hard at it all day he'd been referring to that. But if that had been the case, why hadn't he stopped and spoken to her? Maybe he just hadn't seen her, she thought then she jumped as she realised Dee had been speaking to her.

'You were miles away,' accused Dee. 'Whatever were you thinking about?'

'Nothing much.' Justine forced a smile but when she saw Cal's eyes on her she felt her cheeks grow hot.

'I was just asking if it was all right with you?'

'If what was all right with me?'

Dee looked exasperated. 'Cal saying that he would take us to Altea tomorrow.'

'Oh, yes,' said Justine. 'That's fine by me.' What she didn't add was that by now she felt she would have gone anywhere on earth if it meant being with Cal Douglas.

By the time they'd finished their meal and lingered over coffee the sun had sunk behind the horizon and lights were coming on around the bay while market traders began setting up their stalls along the sea front. As they left the restaurant Justine expressed a desire to dip her toes in the sea.

'You two go on,' said Dee. 'I want to buy some earrings.'

With a wave of her hand she disappeared amongst the throng of people around the stalls and after only a moment's hesitation Cal joined Justine and they strolled down the beach towards the sea.

The sand was still warm from the heat of the sun although by now there was a slight breeze coming in from the sea. Neither spoke until they reached the softly breaking surf, then Justine said quietly, 'Thank you for not giving me away.'

He didn't answer immediately, then he said, 'Why is she so reluctant to talk about this guy? Is he married?'

'Quite possibly, she doesn't know. But she feels foolish.'

'Why should she feel foolish?' Cal kicked off his canvas shoes and bent down to pick them up.

Justine followed his example and gave a blissful sigh as the deliciously cool water lapped around her feet. 'She imagined you would think she was the victim of the classic holiday romance, where some guy promises undying love after a week or so of passion then promptly disappears and is never heard of again.'

'Is that what happened?' He threw her a curious glance then fell into step beside her as they began to walk through the gentle waves.

Justine considered for a moment, 'On the face of it, yes, I suppose so, the only difference being that they weren't on holiday. Dee was at Cowes helping to crew her uncle's boat and Ramon Amador was supposedly representing his firm.'

'Why supposedly?' He turned towards her then before she had a chance to answer he took her hand.

Her spine tingled and for a moment she forgot what she was going to say. Cal however remained silent and she realised he was waiting for her answer. Trying to ignore the overpowering sensation of just being close to him, she attempted to concentrate but Cowes week and Dee's problems seemed a million miles away.

'Ramon told Dee that he worked for

a firm of wine merchants who were one of this year's sponsors at Cowes.'

'And there turned out to be no such firm?' he asked cryptically.

She shook her head. 'Oh yes, the firm existed, they just hadn't heard of Ramon Amador. Dee phoned their office in Valencia — that was who she was phoning from your villa,' she added.

'What did you think of him?'

'Ramon Amador? Oh, I never met him, I've only seen his photograph,' said Justine then added, 'and I have to admit, he's very handsome, I can see what Dee saw in him.'

'But I wouldn't have thought she was the sort of girl to be taken in by a con man,' Cal mused.

Justine sighed. 'That's just it, she isn't usually. But I think she's really fallen for this one, you know love at first sight and all that.'

'And do you believe in all that?' A teasing note had entered his voice and he increased the pressure on her hand.

'I believe you know pretty soon when someone is going to be special,' she replied softly. They strolled on in silence through the soft evening darkness with the dark satin of the water on one side and the twinkling lights of Javea on the other.

Then just when Justine had summoned the courage to ask him about the incident in the church, Cal suddenly stopped, pulling her gently back to him.

Looking down at her he said quietly, 'Is there any chance you may have thought that about me?'

She wasn't sure whether he was still teasing. 'Maybe.' Her voice was little more than a whisper and he had to bend his head to hear.

His cheek brushed hers, she caught the male scent of him, and a glimpse of his profile, the hawk-like features etched against the darkening Spanish sky before his hands encircled her face, lifting it, until his lips covered hers.

His last kiss had been soft, gentle,

teasing but this time he kissed her as if he meant it. A kiss that grew more demanding, a kiss that kindled unknown desires in Justine leaving her breathless and when it was over, helpless with longing.

Even he seemed subdued when he pulled away and for a long while he simply stared down at her upturned face as if in the darkness he was able to read what was in her eyes.

At last he gave a deep sigh. 'You're very lovely, Justine,' he murmured. 'But the last thing I want is for you to get hurt.'

'Why should I get hurt?'

He didn't answer, instead turning his face towards the shoreline and the dark mass of the mountains beyond. There seemed a tension about him as if he knew she waited for a reply.

'I wouldn't like you to find yourself in the same sort of situation as your friend,' he said eventually.

'You mean just another holiday romance?' she asked.

'Something like that, yes.' He nodded.

'And if I said I was fully aware that was all it would be?'

He shifted uncomfortably. 'I still wouldn't want you to be hurt.'

'Are you saying it would be inevitable that you would hurt me?' She reached up and ran her fingers down his cheek.

'I'm saying there could be a very real danger of that.' He caught her hand and pressed it to his lips.

'Let's say I'll cope with that if and when it happens. At this moment I couldn't be happier, so I don't want to worry about what might happen in the future.'

He slid his arm around her and they began to walk up the beach away from the sea to join Dee, and it wasn't until much later when they were in the car climbing back to the villas that Justine realised she still hadn't asked him about the incident in the church.

7

It was dawn and Justine lay listening to the dogs barking in the valley, watching the patterns of light on the ceiling, and thinking about what had happened between her and Cal.

When they had arrived at the villa Dee had tactfully, for once, disappeared indoors leaving her to say goodnight to Cal. He had held her close, kissing her lingeringly before releasing her with a promise to pick them both up at ten the next morning.

She had lain awake most of the night thinking of him. She could hardly believe that she had told him she would agree to a no-strings attached holiday romance when he had said he was afraid of hurting her. It wasn't like her to contemplate such a thing but then, she'd never before met anyone quite like Cal Douglas.

As the first streaks of dawn lightened the sky she had reluctantly come to the conclusion that Cal must be involved with someone else. He had told her there had been someone special but he had indicated that was over, maybe there was someone else now . . . someone who understood the odd hours he worked, someone who didn't mind.

She had as good as condemned Dee for getting involved with Ramon but now she was on the brink of a similar affair and she couldn't help herself.

Even the fact that Dee was uneasy about him, and that they knew little about his background didn't worry her. She had even decided not to pursue the incident in the church. If he hadn't wanted her to see him, that was his business. All she knew was that when she was with him it felt right, when he kissed her it stirred feelings she'd never felt before, and when she wasn't with him she longed for him.

With a sigh she got out of bed and

stood before the open window craning her neck and trying to see more than just the corner of the Casa Rafael that was visible.

There was no sign of life however and Justine padded through to the kitchen to make herself a cup of tea. She knew there was no point in making one for Dee, it was far too early and her friend wouldn't surface for another couple of hours.

She took her tea out to the *naya* and sat in the coolness of the early morning watching the mist slowly clearing in the valley as the sun rose. She wondered what the day would bring forth and what the chances would be of finding Ramon in Altea.

Later after Dee had woken and they had breakfasted on the *naya* she asked her friend what she intended doing when they reached the other town.

Dee hesitated. 'I'm not certain. I might try showing his photograph and making enquiries perhaps in the post office — they must have some sort of electoral roll like we do.'

'But would they be allowed to give that sort of information?' Justine looked doubtful.

Dee shrugged. 'Goodness knows, but I can't think what else I can do.'

'Maybe Cal will have some ideas,' said Justine brightening up just at the sound of his name on her lips.

Dee leaned back in her chair and surveyed her critically through half closed eyes. 'I think you've got it bad over our friend, Mr Douglas,' she observed dryly.

Justine shrugged in what she hoped was a lighthearted manner. 'And what if I have?'

'Nothing . . . it just isn't like you.'

'What isn't?' demanded Justine knowing full well what Dee meant.

'Getting involved with someone you hardly know,' replied Dee bluntly.

'Maybe it's never been the real thing before.'

Dee stared at her. 'And you think this is?'

She shrugged. 'It could be.'

'Oh, Jus, I feel responsible for you and I don't want you to get hurt.'

There it was again. The automatic assumption that she would get hurt. Justine stared at Dee in exasperation. 'Honestly Dee, you're a fine one to talk.'

'I know.' Dee sighed then lifted her head as the sound of a motorbike suddenly filled the air.

'Oh, good God, here she comes already.' Dee stood up. 'I wanted to have a shower before she started organising everything.' With that she disappeared into the bathroom leaving Justine to greet Josephina.

The Spanish woman didn't seem so talkative that morning and when she learned that Dee was in the shower she began work in the kitchen.

When Justine carried their breakfast dishes through Josephina kept her back to her and when Justine attempted further conversation she answered in monosyllables. In the end Justine gave up, deciding to go to her room and get ready for the Altea trip but as she left the kitchen Josephina suddenly called her back.

Glancing at the closed door of the bathroom she asked, 'She find her man?'

Realising that Josephina had probably spoken to her cousin Carlos, Justine smiled and shook her head. 'Not yet. Carlos mentioned Altea,' she added, 'so we're going there today.'

Josephina shook her head and with another almost furtive look at the bathroom door she lowered her voice and muttered, 'He trouble, that one.'

'What do you mean?' Justine stiffened.

'I say no more. But he trouble.' She sniffed and turned back to the sink.

But Justine caught the Spanish woman's arm. 'What do you know about him?' she asked urgently in the same low tone.

'I tell you, I know nothing. Only Carlos, he say that man trouble.' With that she turned away, at the same

132

moment as the bathroom door opened and Dee appeared wrapped in a bath towel. She glanced from Justine to Josephina then back to Justine, then sensing the atmosphere she said, 'Is there anything wrong?'

Josephina carried on with her work and didn't answer and Justine, not wanting Dee to think they had been discussing her, hurriedly shook her head. 'No, nothing,' she said then added, 'If you've finished in there, I think I'll take a cool shower before we go. It's unbearably hot already.'

'It rain later,' said Josephina without turning from the sink.

'Rain?' Dee paused in the doorway and looked over her shoulder in amazement. 'Surely not. It's a beautiful morning, there isn't a cloud in the sky.'

Josephina shrugged her plump shoulders in a resigned fashion and carried on stacking the dishes.

The girls were almost ready when Cal drove onto the drive promptly at ten o'clock. He looked handsome in an open necked white shirt and close fitting rust coloured trousers. He also looked more tanned and the tawny hair was quite bleached as if he'd spent much more time in the sun during the last two days.

Justine's spine tingled when she caught sight of him and as she saw his look of admiration she was pleased she had chosen to wear a cotton sundress with a pretty floral print while her hair she had caught up in a knot allowing the rest to tumble over her shoulders.

Even Dee was looking pretty and feminine in a cotton embroidered shirt tucked into a full gypsy-style skirt.

'Take your sunhats,' said Cal glancing at the vivid blue of the sky. 'It looks as if it's going to be a real scorcher today.'

'Josephina says it's going to rain,' said Dee with a laugh.

'She could well be right,' observed Cal as he opened the car door making it perfectly plain that this time Dee was to travel in the back so that Justine could sit beside him. 'Always take notice of what the locals say, they are usually right.'

Dee pulled a face and climbed into the car while with a surge of happiness Justine took her seat beside Cal. As he started the engine and reversed the car Josephina came out of the villa and stood on the *naya* watching them. Justine waved to her and wondered if she'd also been right about Ramon being trouble.

She hadn't said anything to Dee but she thought she might mention to Cal when they were alone what the Spanish woman had said. They drove out of Javea through vineyards where some of the crop of rich luscious looking fruit was being dried in the sun on large wooden trays, then Cal took the coast road to Altea avoiding the main motorway from Valencia to Alicante.

As he drove he flicked the switch of the car's cassette player and the throbbing sound of Spanish guitar music filled the air. The windows of the car were open and as the breeze caught Justine's long silky hair lifting it from her neck and shoulders she leaned back and closed her eyes. She couldn't remember when she'd been happier and as the heat of the sun caught her face through the windscreen she gave a sigh of pure bliss. Even if her fears proved correct and Cal was involved with someone else, for the time being she didn't care, for he was here beside her and the sun was shining. If it wasn't to last she would have to cope with the misery when the time came but now she was simply going to enjoy what was happening.

Opening her eyes she stole a glance at Cal. He was studying the road ahead, his eyes narrowed against the glare of the sun and as her gaze flickered to the strong brown hands that gripped the wheel she felt a tingle of excitement as she recalled how those hands had held her the night before. As if he sensed her scrutiny he took his eyes from the road, threw her a glance then took one hand from the wheel and covered one of hers where it lay in her lap.

They took their time, stopping for coffee at Calpe, a small fishing town. Justine didn't mind how long it took for she was perfectly happy to be in Cal's company but she sensed that Dee was impatient to get to Altea.

'What's the plan when we get there?' Cal asked casually as they sipped their coffee in a small beachside restaurant. 'Exactly how much do you know about your friend?' He was looking at Dee as he spoke and Justine noticed that she looked uncomfortable.

'To tell you the truth I don't know very much at all. I'm not even sure that he lives there, but I have a photograph of him and I thought I'd start in the local post office in the hopes that someone will recognise him.'

'May I see the photograph?' asked Cal and while Dee fumbled in her bag his eyes met Justine's across the table in quiet assurance that he wouldn't give away that they had discussed Ramon Amador. When Dee handed him the photograph he showed no more than polite interest.

'If I don't have any luck with the post office I suppose I'll just have to rely on local shops,' said Dee and although she tried to sound positive, Justine detected a hopeless note in her voice and her heart ached for her friend. She knew she would be heartbroken if she was forced to return to England without having found Ramon. As they approached Altea they noticed an increase in the volume of traffic. Moments later they saw the reason. Brightly coloured bunting was hung above the streets and flags fluttered from every building while crowds of people thronged the pavements and impatient car drivers found themselves stuck in an ever-growing snarl-up of traffic. A cacophony of car horns, music and human voices filled the air mingling with the aromas of food from take-away vans, ice cream and the ever pervading smell of fish.

'It must be one of their fiestas,' said Cal as he stuck his head out of the car window in an attempt to see what was happening ahead.

'How exciting,' Justine craned her neck eagerly. 'Do you think there'll be a parade of Moors and Christians like it said in the paper, Cal?'

'I wouldn't be surprised, they seem to have parades at the drop of a hat. The immediate problem is going to be finding somewhere to park . . .'

They eventually found somewhere although it was some way out of town, then together with several hundred other people who seemed to have had the same idea they walked back into Altea.

'This isn't going to help in your search for Ramon,' said Cal to Dee.

She nodded grimly. 'I was thinking the same thing. But I still think I'll try the post office first.'

They had to battle their way through

the crowds in the centre of the town and while Dee joined the queue inside the post office Justine and Cal waited outside.

'I don't think she stands a hope in hell in this crowd,' he commented.

'You can't blame her for trying though, can you?' said Justine.

He looked down at her and their eyes met and it was as if they were the only two in the town square. 'No,' he murmured with a smile. 'I'm beginning to understand how she feels.'

'I hope she finds him,' said Justine, but when Dee joined them again, one look at her face told them she hadn't got anywhere. She tried showing his photograph in one or two shops but people seemed more interested in what was going on in the street than in looking at photographs.

At last Cal intervened; he had been talking to a group of elderly men sitting in the town square and as he returned he said, 'There is going to be a parade of Moors and Christians but not until later. There are other activities going on at the beach so I suggest we make our way down there, get something to eat then we can come back here later and find a place to watch the parade.'

They managed to find a pleasant spot on the beach in the shelter of the wall of a beach café shaded from the sun by a mass of almond trees. Cal bought some food and drink from a take-away van and they picnicked while watching water sports in the bay. Justine would have been totally happy just being so close to Cal if she hadn't been aware of Dee's growing frustration. It grew even hotter and they took a brief siesta then when Justine awoke it was to find groups of people in elaborate costumes making their way along the seafront and into the town.

'Look,' she called to the other two. 'Those people must be going to take part in the parade — there are dozens of them.'

Cal nodded and stood up brushing the sand from his clothes. 'The local people consider it a great honour to be picked to take part in these parades, it's a very important part of their heritage and culture.'

'I suppose all this is part of the research you've done,' Justine commented as they made their way back into the town. 'I must confess,' she continued when Cal didn't reply, 'I don't know very much about Spanish history although I had heard of the Moors and the Christians. You must be an authority on it, Cal. You'll have to explain what is going on.'

'Oh God,' groaned Dee. 'Not another history lesson.'

'Don't worry, I'll spare you that,' Cal grinned but Justine got the sudden impression that he didn't know any more than she did. Then she told herself not to be so stupid, after all Cal's subject was early Spanish history.

'It was bad enough yesterday,' Dee went on, 'what with Justine and her saints and churches, I left her to it in the end.'

Justine stole a look at Cal but his expression remained inscrutable and then they were caught up in the throng of people lining the streets and the moment was lost.

The sky had become overcast and the heat was oppressive and Justine found herself remembering what Josephina had said about rain and she glanced anxiously at the sky.

They found a spot in the town square behind rows of chairs which were already filled with local families. Within minutes more people came to stand behind them and in a short time they were completely hemmed in by the crowd. As the anticipation of the people grew the atmosphere became almost electric, the sky darkened and Justine thought she might faint from the heat and the feeling of claustrophobia.

When she thought she couldn't bear it for another moment, Cal, sensing her discomfort, slid his arm around her waist and she leaned thankfully against him. Moments later they heard the first throbbing beat of drums and the ripple of excitement in the crowd grew as the word spread like wildfire that the parade was on its way.

Justine wasn't sure what she had been expecting but as the first of the parade came into view she felt the thrill of some primitive urge. A line of women in identical Moorish costumes stretched the width of the road. Their movement, a swaying motion was slow and deliberate and they progressed only inches at a time. Their costumes consisted of harem trousers of gold cloth, red embroidered tunics, plumed headdresses of emerald green and Moorish slippers of gold, the toes pointed and curled.

'Oh look,' gasped Justine. 'They're magnificent.'

'Got your camera?' said Cal, but Justine was already busily taking photographs.

'Don't get too carried away,' said Cal

144

warningly. 'There'll be hundreds more.' And he was right for behind that first line of women there followed a line of men in full Moorish battle costume with white trousers and tunics, black and scarlet cloaks, metal helmets with white plumes each carrying a vicious looking spear. Even Dee seemed impressed and she also began taking photographs.

After that there followed line after line of men and women and sometimes even children, with each line it seemed trying to outdo the one before in spectacle and magnificence.

Each section had its leader, a beautiful woman or a noble warrior proud to have been chosen to lead and playing unashamedly to the crowds encouraging more and more appreciation and applause.

And throughout it all the whole parade throbbed to the accompaniment of dozens of musicians who followed the lines of warriors. To the underlying beat of huge kettledrums pulled along by small boys was added the higher pitched sounds of flutes, trumpets and clarinets all building up into what would eventually be one huge crescendo. Justine wasn't certain when it dawned on her that each of these groups were playing the same tune and she was about to mention the fact to Cal when a mass of chariots pulled by black horses came into view. The warriors in these chariots were in costumes of black, silver and midnight blue and the overall effect was so stunning that the crowd surged forward as people jostled for positions to take photographs.

For a moment Justine found her view completely obscured and with a cry she thrust her camera into Cal's hands. 'Oh, please, Cal, get a shot of that,' she gasped.

He grasped her camera and pushing his way through the crowd crouched down in front of the oncoming chariots and took several pictures.

He was grinning as he forged his way back to her side then as he handed her the camera the smile

suddenly disappeared from his face.
Justine frowned as he looked around.

'Where's Dee?'

Justine spun round but Dee wasn't
standing in the spot where she had
been throughout the parade. Wildly
she looked but all she could see was
a mass of unfamiliar Spanish faces and
no sign of her friend.

8

At first Justine wasn't too alarmed for as she pointed out to Cal, Dee was well able to take care of herself. It was Cal who seemed the most worried and again Justine felt a twinge of jealousy at his apparent concern for Dee. When half an hour of searching still revealed no sign of Dee even Justine began to wonder.

The parade was still going on but it had lost its magic, then at last they found themselves on the fringe of the crowd.

'Maybe we should make our way back to the car before this crowd begins to move,' said Cal then added, 'There's always the chance that Dee may also have done that. She knows where the car is and that we would eventually end up there.'

Justine agreed but as they made their

way through the now deserted streets she felt annoyed that probably through Dee's selfishness they had been forced to cut short their fun.

They finally reached the car to find a note attached to the windscreen. Justine snatched it up and scanning it, tossed it at Cal saying, 'What did I tell you? She's found Ramon and gone off with him. She says not to worry and not to wait — he will take her home.'

Cal frowned and read the note himself then without a word got into the car and leaning across opened the passenger door at the same moment as hordes of people began surging through the street towards them.

'The parade's over,' said Cal switching on the ignition. 'Let's get out of here before we get caught up in the rush.'

They drove in silence until they had left Altea behind and were out on the open road. It was Justine who broke the strained silence. 'She must have seen him in the crowd, gone after him then not been able to get back to us.'

When Cal didn't reply she threw him an uneasy glance and was dismayed to find his face set. Haltingly she went on, 'Don't you think that's what happened?'

He gave a shrug and without taking his eyes from the road he said, 'That's one explanation . . .'

'But not what you think happened?'

'It was strange that at the one moment when my . . . when our attention was diverted she chose to slip away.'

'But why should she do that?' Justine frowned. 'I don't understand what you're getting at, Cal.'

'It's nothing,' he said quickly then when he caught sight of her expression he added, 'There's just been so much mystery surrounding this guy, we spend so long searching for him, then when he does decide to put in an appearance, we miss it.'

Justine bit her lip but was forced to

agree then she went on to tell him what Josephina had said.

He threw her a quick glance. 'And you didn't tell Dee that Josephina said this guy was trouble?'

Justine shook her head miserably. 'No, I didn't. But if I had, Dee wouldn't have believed it, you've seen what she's like and when she's set on something, nothing will stop her.'

They fell silent again as they travelled towards Javea. It was dark by now, but still oppressively hot and great banks of cloud had built up to produce a gloomy starless night.

When they had almost reached the road to the villas Justine said, 'I'm sorry, Cal that you've had all this to put up with. After all, Dee isn't your problem. I promise you we won't bother you with it again.'

He drove into the drive of the Casa Rafael without answering then switching off the engine he leaned across and pulled Justine roughly into his arms and before she had a chance to say more he brought his mouth down firmly over hers.

With a sigh she gave herself up to the luxury of feeling his arms around her and in that instant she forgot Dee and her problems, wanting only to concentrate on what was happening to her.

The kiss lasted a long time evoking desires deep inside Justine she'd hardly dreamt were there then Cal drew away from her, and said, 'Let's go inside.'

She followed him up the spiral staircase pausing when they reached the top while he kissed her again. By this time Justine was feeling heady with longing but she was also aware they were quite alone in the Casa Rafael. She had already indicated to Cal that she was living for the moment and as she watched him unlock the door she realised anything could happen.

She knew she was acting out of character but she also knew she was hopelessly in love with Cal Douglas. Although his warning that she would get hurt had reverberated in her head for the last twenty four hours it made no difference to the way she felt as they walked through the lounge and Cal opened the glass doors to the upstairs *naya*.

It was hot and airless, the shrubs and plants on the *naya* motionless as the sweet heady scent of jasmine enveloped them. Cal sat down on one of the luxurious sun loungers and as Justine looked down at him he stretched out his hand, took hers and gently pulled her down beside him. With a sigh she slid her arm round his neck resting her head against his chest. He held her closely for a long time so that she could hear the steady beating of his heart. Then suddenly he lifted his head and appeared to be listening.

'What is it?' she asked watching the sharp outline of his profile.

'That noise,' he replied.

She too then lifted her head from his chest and listened to what sounded like a rustling of foliage.

'It's raining,' he said.

'So Josephina was right.' Justine silently hoped that was the only thing the Spanish woman had been right about. She laid her head against his chest again and they listened to the rain as it pattered on the leaves and plopped into the pool, both of them content to lie close, to be alone for the first time.

It was Cal who stirred first and gently began tracing his fingers down her cheek. She lifted her face and gazed up at him. A single lamp was burning in the room behind them so she could only see his silhouette.

'You know, Justine,' he murmured, 'you really are very lovely. That guy must have been crazy dropping you for a Swedish girl.'

'I expect she had masses of blonde hair and legs that go on for ever,' said Justine ruefully. 'They usually are like that, Swedish girls.' As she thought of Gary she was amazed that it didn't hurt.

'Maybe they are,' said Cal. 'I wouldn't know, that's not my type.'

'I thought all gentlemen preferred blondes.'

'Well here's one who doesn't,' he whispered against her ear. 'It takes a dark, exotic woman to turn me on, but on the other hand, maybe I'm no gentleman.' With a deep husky laugh he slid his free hand into the dark mass of her long silky hair tilting her jaw towards him until his lips found hers again.

Her mouth parted beneath his welcoming him as their kiss progressed from a simple meeting of lips to a delicious exploration becoming more demanding with every passing second. He allowed his hand to move from her hair, caressing her shoulder moving down her body, moulding her hip which sent shudders of delight coursing through her, then moving lightly over her thigh covered only by the thin silky fabric of her sundress.

Gently, sensually he stroked her leg

taking his time over every movement until her nerves were taut with unleashed desire then his mouth released hers, and he began kissing the vulnerable hollow between her neck and her shoulder.

Justine gasped as she felt him harden with desire beneath her and as she tilted her head anticipating further delights she felt him begin to undo the buttons at the front of her sundress. She did nothing to stop him because she wanted this as much as he did. She refused to think whatever heartbreak there might be to come; all she knew was that she was there with Cal and that she loved him. The front of her sundress parted revealing the swell of her breast and as Cal released the clasp at the front of her lacy bra she heard him catch his breath. But when his hand cupped her breast, his fingers caressing her hardening nipple it was her turn to stiffen with uncontrollable desire.

His lips found hers again then he lowered his head to her breasts and with lips and tongue he aroused her to undreamed of heights. She felt him move beneath her and give a slight groan as if he were having difficulty restraining his own desire then suddenly there came the sound of a car door being closed and they both froze.

As they listened they heard voices then a car started up and went away down the hill. All was silent then they heard Dee's voice.

'Justine,' she called. 'Are you there?'

'Damn her,' muttered Cal while Justine felt her heart sink in bitter disappointment.

'Are you over there, Jus? Cal?'

Justine gave a deep sigh. 'Yes, Dee,' she called, 'we're here.'

'Shall I come over?' called Dee. 'I'm getting soaked in this rain but I've got so much to tell you, I can hardly wait.'

It was Cal who answered. 'We'll be over in a few minutes, Dee,' he said abruptly.

There was silence then Dee said, 'Oh . . . all right.'

They stood up and Justine buttoned her sundress. 'Cal . . . I'm sorry . . .'

He drew her into his arms and held her close. 'It's all right,' he whispered. 'It wasn't your fault and,' he hesitated . . . 'who knows, maybe it's for the best.'

She leaned back and looked at him in the half light. 'No Cal,' she said sharply, 'I don't want you to feel that way.'

He shook his head and half turned away from her but she took hold of his shoulders almost forcing her to look at him again. 'You wanted to, Cal, I know you did,' she said quietly.

He sighed and stared down at her then his arms tightened around her. 'Of course I did . . . but I don't want you to . . .'

'I know,' she interrupted, 'you don't want me to get hurt. You said that and I've accepted it. I don't know what it is that will cause you to hurt me, but I'll cope with it when the time comes, now, I just want to enjoy our time together.'

He lowered his head and kissed her and she closed her eyes, briefly yearning for what hadn't happened. Then gently extricating herself from his arms she said, 'We'd better go and hear what Dee has to tell us, that is, if you want to, Cal, you don't have to.'

'Yes I do,' he replied grimly as he switched off the table lamp, 'I want to know the reasons for my disrupted day.'

They ran together through the torrential rain and arrived wet and breathless at the villa where they found Dee in the kitchen brewing tea.

'What's that, a peace offering?' asked Cal, as he dried his hair with the towel Justine gave him.

'Am I in your bad books?' asked Dee trying to look contrite but failing miserably because of her flushed face and shining eyes.

'Let's say we were a bit concerned when you vanished so dramatically,' he replied with a note of sarcasm in his voice.

Dee pouted then turned away to pour the tea. 'I thought you might have been glad of some time to yourselves without me tagging along,' she said.

'We were,' replied Cal in the same tone, 'until you shouted out just now.'

'Oh dear,' Dee put the teapot down and stared from one to the other of them. 'I'm sorry,' she said and for once she sounded as if she meant it, then immediately she brightened again, 'It was incredible,' she went on. 'You'll never believe it.'

'Try us,' said Cal as they carried their mugs of tea to the lounge and settled themselves in the cane chairs.

'Yes,' said Justine who had been quiet until then, 'we want to know, Dee, how did you meet up with Ramon?'

'It was chance . . . sheer chance. It was while we were watching the parade — I suddenly saw him. I couldn't believe my eyes but he was there on the opposite side of the road, he was behind the crowd and he was walking up the hill. I knew I had to move fast if I was going to catch him.'

'Why didn't you tell us?' asked Justine glancing swiftly at Cal as she recalled the comment he had made about Dee deliberately giving them the slip. His expression however was inscrutable as he waited for her reply.

'I tried to,' replied Dee 'but you were so caught up with getting pictures of those chariots that I couldn't attract your attention. I knew if I left things any longer I would miss Ramon altogether so I just ran. As it was I had to get through the parade to cross the road and then through the crowd on the opposite side, and I still had to run up the hill before I caught up with him.'

'I expect you gave him quite a shock,' remarked Cal drily as he drained his mug.

'Oh yes,' Dee sighed. 'He couldn't believe his eyes when he saw me. We tried to talk but the music was so loud that in the end he drew me into a side alley where it was quieter. By the time we went back to look for you,

you'd gone. I explained to Ramon where we'd left the car and he took me there in his car, then we spent the rest of the evening just catching up . . . ' she trailed off but her eyes were shining again leaving them in no doubt what form this catching up had taken. When they remained silent Dee looked at both of them then her expression changed and with a sudden frown she said, 'I know what you're both thinking, but it wasn't like that, everything was fine, honestly it was.'

'So what was his explanation for not contacting you?' asked Justine quietly.

'Oh, he's had personal problems which he has been trying to sort out,' replied Dee airily. 'One of which was his job. He'd been made redundant from that wine merchants. That must have been what they were trying to tell me when I phoned, but what with my Spanish being so poor I must have misunderstood them.'

'Does he live in Altea?' asked Cal.

'He shares a flat there with two other

Spaniards,' said Dee. 'But would you believe for the past week he's been helping a friend to re-fit a boat right here in the port at Javea? All that time I've been looking for him he's been here right under my nose.'

'So when are you seeing him again?' asked Justine.

'Tomorrow.' Dee stretched happily. 'We're going out in the evening but I may just go and see him on this boat during the day.' She glanced up as if she had suddenly become aware of the others. 'Have you two got any plans for tomorrow?'

It was Cal who replied, not giving Justine time to answer but at his reply she felt a twinge of disappointment.

'I have work to do,' he said, 'but I have to go into Javea first so I'll run you down to the port.'

'Oh thanks,' said Dee finishing her tea and standing up, 'that way Justine can meet Ramon.' Humming softly to herself she disappeared into the kitchen leaving Justine and Cal looking at each other across the table.

'Well,' she said when she was sure Dee was out of earshot, 'what did you make of all that?'

Cal stood up. 'I don't know.' Walking round the table he put his hands on her shoulders and stared down at her, 'But she seems happy enough . . . for the present anyway.' Then gently kissing her forehead, he said, 'I'd better be going, Justine, it's been quite a day.'

She lifted her face, wanting him to kiss her again, but he didn't, and as she watched him go out of the door and run lightly down the steps, she felt as if the magic between them had vanished. For a long while she stood on the *naya* staring towards the Casa Rafael. The rain had stopped as abruptly as it had started and the night air felt fresh and cool after the oppressive heat. At last she sighed and turned away. As Cal had said, it had been quite a day.

She was about to enter her bedroom when Dee called out. She opened the door of Dee's room and found her friend sitting on the bed.

'I say, Jus, did I interrupt something between you and Cal? Oh God, I'm sorry,' she said when she caught sight of Justine's expression. 'I just didn't think, I was so excited at finding Ramon and I was bursting to tell you . . . I am sorry,' she said again.

'It's all right,' said Justine wearily, pushing back her hair. 'I'm glad you found him, Dee, I really am. It must have been a relief to know nothing had happened to him.'

Dee nodded and her eyes sparkled, 'I also found out he isn't married.'

'Well, I'm glad,' said Justine thinking that it seemed as if Josephina and Carlos had been wrong about Ramon.

'Oh, Justine,' called Dee, 'there's one other thing I think might interest you.'

Justine stopped. There was something about Dee's tone that put her on guard.

'You remember I said I thought I'd

seen Cal Douglas before?'

Justine nodded for her throat seemed to have gone dry.

'Today it suddenly came to me where it was.'

Justine stared wordlessly at Dee waiting for her to go on.

'It must have been being with Ramon again that jogged my memory, you see it was when I was with Ramon before that I saw Cal.'

'What do you mean?' Justine stared at her.

'It was at Cowes. He was standing on one of the marinas, leaning on the rail.'

'But he couldn't have been,' said Justine in bewilderment.

'I can assure you he was. We'd been on my uncle's boat for best part of the evening,' she smiled at the memory, 'and when we eventually came up, he was standing there on the marina. He even had to move for us to pass him.'

'Dee, you must have been mistaken,'

cried Justine. 'It couldn't possibly have been Cal. Don't you remember, when we first met him and we said we came from the Isle of Wight, we asked if he'd ever been there and he said only once when he was a boy and he'd stayed at Shanklin?'

'That may have been what he said,' replied Dee grimly, 'but I know I wasn't mistaken. There's something very distinctive about that mass of hair and those eyes ... Justine, you're not getting too involved are you?' She stretched out her hand but Justine ignored it. 'I think you should be very careful,' Dee went on when Justine remained silent, 'After all, you don't know anything about him.'

'My God, Dee, you're a fine one to talk!' exploded Justine. 'How much did you know about your Spanish friend? Very little but that didn't stop you getting involved.'

'I know, I know,' Dee held up her hands as if to fend Justine off. 'But like I said, I brought you here and I feel responsible.'

'Well, don't. I'm not a child, Dee and I'm perfectly capable of taking care of myself,' Justine retorted angrily then she stormed out of the room slamming the door behind her.

9

Justine hardly slept, her mind in turmoil about what Dee had said. Her immediate reaction had been to tell Dee she was mistaken but since then, doubts had crept in.

Suppose Dee had seen Cal at Cowes? What had he been doing there and why had he lied when he said he hadn't been there since he was a boy? From the way Dee had described the incident it sounded as if Cal would have seen her when she and Ramon passed him on the marina, but when they'd first arrived in Javea, he'd shown no sign of recognition.

Justine tossed and turned then finally fell into an uneasy sleep only to be woken a couple of hours later by the sound of a car. She jumped out of bed and crossing to the window was in time to see the rear lights of a car leave the Casa Rafael and disappear down the hill. She flicked on her bedside light to find that it was only three o'clock. Why was Cal going out at that time and where on earth could he be going? She lay down and stared at the ceiling. There were so many unanswered questions and she knew in her heart that sooner or later she was going to have to tackle Cal.

There had been the incident in the church which she had done nothing about and now, the deliberate lie about his visits to the Isle of Wight. That's if it really had been a lie, she thought, and not just a case of mistaken identity on Dee's part.

Her thoughts switched to Dee and in spite of her anguish she smiled in the darkness for although they'd argued there had been something infectious about her friend's happiness in finding Ramon. Justine hoped the reasons he'd given for not contacting Dee had been genuine and that he wasn't about to hurt her again. As she thought of

Ramon and Dee together her thoughts inevitably returned to Cal. She'd never met anyone like him, with the power to leave her helpless with longing with just a glance from those unusual golden eyes. She knew if they hadn't been interrupted by Dee they would have made love, making a mockery of her usual code of morals.

In the past it would have been unthinkable for Justine to make love with someone she'd known for barely a week. She had condemned Dee for doing the same thing and she could now only put such recklessness down to the fact that she, and very possibly Dee, were really in love for the first time in their lives.

Dee had had hordes of admirers but Justine doubted she had ever found real love while she, had had so few, and even with Gary, whom she had believed she had really loved, she had never known what she now felt for Cal.

At last she fell into another fitful sleep and when she awoke it was to find the room flooded with sunlight. She lay for a moment trying to collect her thoughts then she dragged herself to the window. Cal's Renault was parked in its usual place at the side of the Casa Rafael.

After making two mugs of tea she tapped on Dee's door. Surprisingly she found her friend wide awake. Not giving her a chance to say anything she set the mug down on her bedside table saying, 'I'm sorry I was so snappy last night, Dee.'

'I was thinking the same thing,' said Dee with a rueful smile. 'Don't take any notice what I said about Cal . . . maybe I was mistaken.'

'Maybe,' agreed Justine, 'maybe not. But I'd appreciate it if you didn't say anything to him. I'll ask him myself when the occasion arises.'

'OK,' Dee nodded, then sipping her tea she changed the subject. 'You will come down to the port and meet Ramon this morning?' she asked eagerly and when Justine nodded she added, 'I shouldn't think we'd be able to stay long as he'll be working, so we can go on the beach afterwards.'

'Good idea,' replied Justine. 'But first I'd like a dip in the pool. It feels fresh and cool out there after that rain last night.'

After their swim they breakfasted then dressed in shorts and suntops and were ready when Cal backed the Renault out of the Casa Rafael. This time Dee automatically climbed into the back leaving Justine to take her place beside Cal. As she closed her door Justine threw Cal a glance and her pulses raced when she saw how handsome he looked in denim shorts and tee shirt. He gave her a brief smile but she was unable to see his eyes which were hidden behind dark glasses.

They drove through the orange groves into the town and as they approached the port Justine became aware of Dee's growing anticipation.

'Do you know where to find Ramon?'

she asked over her shoulder.

'I have a pretty good idea,' replied Dee. 'You can drop us off where you like, Cal,' she added.

They stopped on the wharf a few yards from the moorings where dozens of yachts were berthed.

'Why don't you go and see if you can find him while Justine and I wait here,' said Cal climbing from the car.

Dee hesitated then said, 'All right, I'll give you a shout Jus, when I find the right boat.' Then she was gone, running lightly across the wharf her golden hair gleaming in the sunlight.

Cal sat down on the sea wall and indicated for Justine to join him. They sat very close together and after a while Cal slipped his arm round her and she rested her head on his shoulder happy just to be close to him but wishing that they could spend the day together. They remained silent looking out over the busy port, the fishing fleet on the far wharf ready to put to sea at the turn of the tide, and the yachts gently tugging at their moorings. Then Justine became aware that Cal had lowered his head and was watching her.

'What were you thinking about?' he asked. 'You were miles away.'

She gave a rueful smile. 'I was, literally. I was thinking how like my home all this is,' she waved her hand to indicate the port and the boats, then apprehensively she waited to see if he agreed but he remained silent. She threw him an anxious glance but his expression was inscrutable as he narrowed his eyes against the sun and stared out to sea. Impulsively she reached a decision. 'Cal, when we first met you, you said you'd only been to the Isle of Wight once, when you were a boy.'

Slowly he turned his head and as his eyes met hers she felt her spine tingle as she remembered how he had aroused her the night before.

'That's right,' he replied evenly and when she was forced to lower her gaze in confusion, he added quietly, 'Why?'

She swallowed. 'Dee said she thought she'd seen you somewhere before, then last night she told me that she'd remembered it was at Cowes.'

Slowly he withdrew his arm from her shoulders. 'I can't imagine what made her think that.' He spoke lightly but Justine detected an unfamiliar edge to his voice.

'She said it was when she was with Ramon that she thought she saw you and that seeing him again yesterday probably jogged her memory.' She hesitated then added, 'I told her she must have been mistaken.'

'Absolutely,' he replied firmly. Then shielding his eyes from the sun, he said, 'Look, isn't that Dee waving over there. I think she's trying to attract your attention.'

They stood up and Justine put on her sunglasses and peered across the marina. 'That must be the yacht, the one with the blue pennants. I suppose

I'd better go round there.'

'You don't sound too keen,' he commented.

'I'm not,' she replied simply. 'I'd much rather stay with you.'

He stood very still, his face turned away from her and her heart lurched painfully when he didn't reply. Was he having second thoughts about their relationship? The idea was unbearable and Justine touched his arm and said, 'I know you said you have work to do, but will I see you later, Cal? Dee will be going out with Ramon,' she added holding her breath as she waited for his reply.

'Yes,' he said and kissed her lightly on the lips, 'I'll see you later,' then with a brief smile he was gone, striding across the wharf to his car.

She watched him, puzzled by his manner for she had felt that his smile had held a touch of sadness.

He started the engine then with a wave he pulled away and the car joined the traffic heading for the town. She wondered why he hadn't taken the shorter coast road back to the villa if he was anxious to get to work, then with a sigh she began to walk along the wharf to join Dee.

She passed several large luxurious yachts, some with their owners working aboard or simply lazing on the decks, others seemingly deserted. When she reached Dee she found her flushed and bright eyed so she knew she'd found Ramon, a fact that was confirmed as the dark-eyed Spaniard she had seen in the photograph suddenly appeared on the deck of the large white yacht moored behind Dee.

'Justine, this is Ramon,' said Dee unnecessarily. Then turning to him she added, 'Ramon, this is my friend, Justine.'

He smiled and nodded at Justine and she decided he was even more handsome in the flesh with his dark hair, almost black eyes and very white teeth. He wore only a pair of red shorts which revealed his lean deeply tanned body. Justine could see immediately why Dee found him so attractive but she also guessed that Ramon Amador was only too aware of his charm.

He indicated for them to join him and as she stepped aboard Justine noticed a man working on the far deck. It looked as if he was varnishing part of the woodwork but he didn't look up as they followed Ramon below. In the galley they found another man, an older Spaniard who glared at the sudden intrusion. Ramon spoke to him in rapid Spanish and muttering to himself, the man disappeared into a cabin beyond the galley pulling the sliding door shut behind him. Ramon shrugged apologetically then smiled and gestured for the girls to sit down, while he opened a cupboard above the small sink and produced a bottle of red wine and some glasses.

Justine was about to protest that it was far too early to start drinking, but something stopped her and meekly she accepted the glass that Ramon handed her.

'Dee tell me about you,' he said. 'You like my country? *Si*?'

'Very much,' replied Justine wondering why she suddenly felt nervous. 'It's beautiful.'

'Justine loves your old buildings and churches,' explained Dee. 'But me, well I just love the sun . . . oh and the people of course,' she added and they all laughed. It was however a polite laugh followed by a strained silence and Justine struggled to find something to say.

They continued to drink their wine with the odd snatches of stilted conversation usually instigated by Dee, then Justine in desperation asked Ramon if he had enjoyed Cowes week.

He frowned and stared into the glass and for one unbelievable moment Justine thought he too was going to deny ever having been to Cowes, then he lifted his glass to the light twirling the stem so that the remains of the wine swirled in the bottom of the glass.

She stared at him waiting for his reply and it was as he lifted the bottle to refill their glasses that they heard noises above deck.

Ramon raised his head listening intently, then there came a series of thuds followed by the sound of running footsteps.

'Whatever's happening?' gasped Dee but Ramon was on his feet as the door between the galley and the cabin burst open and the older man appeared. He shouted something roughly to Ramon and they both turned towards the stairs to the deck, but before either of them had time to move, the noises above were mingled with the sounds of shouting, and before the girls had time to think what was happening or to even be afraid, three armed Spanish policemen burst down the steps into the galley.

The next few moments were terrifying as Ramon and the other man struggled, were overpowered then marched up onto the deck. But worse was to come, for as Justine and Dee watched in horrified bewilderment it soon became obvious that they too were to be included in the arrest.

The police took no notice of their protests and they were marched along the wharf to two waiting police vans. The three men were bundled into the back of one and the girls into another.

'Dee, what the hell is happening?' Justine's voice came out as barely more than a hoarse whisper.

'I wish I knew,' muttered Dee.

The policeman who accompanied them motioned for them to be silent but Dee, ignored this. 'Where are you taking us? What are we supposed to have done?' she demanded. He answered predictably in Spanish, neither girls having a clue what he said, but it seemed they were not to have long to wait to learn their fate for very soon they stopped outside a large white building and they were ordered out of the van and into what Justine assumed was the local police station.

They were taken to some sort of reception area with many rooms and passages leading from it. It was sparsely furnished with one huge desk, a few chairs and two large overhead fans that whirred noisily. For one wild moment Justine was reminded of films she'd seen where innocent tourists were interrogated, made the victims of some foreign regime and locked away for years. She felt a wave of hysteria then as the room seemed to tilt alarmingly she forced herself to get a grip on her panic. A bout of hysterics wouldn't help either of them.

Ramon and the other two men were dragged off in one direction and Justine couldn't help but notice that not once did Ramon as much as glance at Dee. When it became apparent that they too were about to be frogmarched away Dee suddenly shook off the hands of the policeman who was holding her and striding across to the large desk she addressed herself to the man who was sitting behind it.

'We are British,' she said imperiously drawing herself up to her full height and glaring down at him. 'We demand to know what is happening and why we have been brought here.'

He in turn stared calmly up at her. He was small and fat, balding with a thick black moustache. There was a shrewd expression in his dark eyes. 'You will be charged in due course,' he replied in heavily accented English.

'What do you mean, charged?' demanded Dee. 'Charged with what? We haven't done anything for God's sake!'

The man shrugged and indicated for the policemen to take the girls away.

They were led away with Dee loudly protesting that she wanted to see someone from the British Embassy. Worse was to come, when to Justine's dismay, they were taken to separate rooms and as the door of her room slammed behind her she again had to fight a wave of panic.

Trying to control herself and overcome her fear she stared at the closed door then in growing desperation she turned and looked at the room. It too was sparsely furnished, with a folding bed along one wall, a table and a chair. The one small window was set too high in the wall for her to see out and the room seemed to be soundproofed for she couldn't hear any of the bustle outside.

She sank down onto the bed trying to control the waves of panic so that she could concentrate on trying to reason out what was happening. Obviously a mistake had been made and she and Dee had been wrongly arrested. Whether Ramon and the other men had also been wrongly arrested she had no idea, but at that moment she wasn't too worried about them. The main problem was convincing the Spanish police that they were simply British holidaymakers and had done no wrong. But who could convince them if they wouldn't listen? For a moment Justine felt close to despair then she thought of Cal. Of course! When he couldn't find them, he would surely report their disappearance to the police. Immediately her spirits rose. Cal would come to their rescue.

Then she frowned. Had Cal said he would come to the beach to pick them up? She couldn't remember, but somehow she didn't think he had. Her heart sank again. But when they didn't return to Las Bellotas he would surely become concerned. But that would not be until evening and it was still only mid-morning.

She stood up and dragged the chair to the window but even by standing on it on tiptoe she was unable to see out. She wondered where Dee was and climbing off the chair again she knocked on first one, then the other wall but there was no reassuring, answering knock. Sitting down on the bed again she came to a decision. As soon as anyone appeared she would ask them to contact Cal at the Casa Rafael.

She felt better once she'd made a positive decision but it was several agonising hours later before she heard the bolt being drawn on the door.

She looked up sharply, mentally bracing herself to do battle with the Spanish policeman then as the door swung open she stared.

Cal stood in the doorway.

With a cry Justine started to her feet and over-whelmed by a surge of relief, she hurled herself at him.

'Oh, Cal,' she gasped. 'You came. I knew you would.'

Lightly he held her as she buried her face in his chest, her tears flowing with the sudden release of tension.

'But how did you know where we were?' she asked after a while and lifting her head to look up into his face she became aware, over his shoulder of the grinning face of the policeman in the passage behind him. At the same instant she realised there was something strange about Cal's manner. Although he was holding her, it wasn't the loving embrace she'd come to expect from him, instead, it was how an adult would hold a child and there had not been one word of comfort or endearment.

'Cal?' she stared at him but there was a strangely shuttered expression on his face as if he couldn't bring himself to look at her. She clutched his arms, 'Cal, what is it? What's wrong, please tell me?' Despair was back in her voice and he allowed his eyes to meet hers. What she saw bewildered her even more. His expression, at first blank changed as he looked at her and she saw again the sadness that she'd seen earlier. 'Cal . . . ?' she began again then stopped as he turned to the door and kicked it shut in the face of the grinning Spaniard. Turning back to Justine he took her by the shoulders gently guiding her to the bed and when she was sitting he looked down at her.

'Justine,' he said at last, and his voice sounded unusually husky. 'There's something I have to explain.'

She stared up at him her large dark eyes growing trustingly wider so that he was forced again to glance away.

'Things aren't quite what they seem.'

She gave a shaky laugh. 'You can say that again . . .'

'No,' he interrupted, 'you don't understand. I'm not who you think.'

She continued to stare at him not understanding but certain that he would sort everything out. She gave a tremulous smile. 'What are you trying to tell me, that your name isn't Cal Douglas? That perhaps you're some film star in disguise?' She joked in an attempt to lighten the tension.

He shook his head. 'No, my name is Douglas,' he drew a small wallet from the back pocket of his shorts and held it open so that she could see it, 'but I'm not a writer. I'm a Detective Sergeant with the CID.'

10

Justine stared at him in amazement but because she was feeling so relieved she felt no immediate alarm. Instead she smiled and said, 'I always thought there was a mystery about you, but I suppose when you're off-duty and on holiday it's up to you what you do.'

He frowned then slowly shook his head. 'You don't understand. I'm not off-duty and I'm not on holiday.'

'You're not?' she smiled up at him. 'In that case perhaps you can exert your powers on our Spanish friends and tell them to let us go. God knows why we were brought here in the first place. But what I don't understand, Cal, is how did you know we were here?'

Ignoring her question he sat astride the chair, his arms resting on its back facing her as she sat on the bed. 'Justine, I have spent the last few hours negotiating your release.'

Her eyes widened in astonishment. 'But I haven't been charged with anything, at least I don't think I have, unless it was done in Spanish or behind my back.'

'No, there was nothing like that but you were going to come in for some pretty intensive questioning.'

'But what about?'

'I think I've convinced them you are unable to help and that by questioning you, they would be wasting their time.' He paused, then staring intently at her, he said, 'I hope my faith in you isn't misplaced.'

'Of course it isn't,' she cried in bewilderment. 'I just wish I knew what we're supposed to have done.' When he remained silent she leaned forward and said urgently, 'Are they going to let us go?'

He nodded. 'Yes . . .'

She breathed a sigh of relief. 'Well, thank God for that . . .'

'But there are a couple of conditions . . .'

'What conditions?' she looked up sharply.

'That you return to England with me first thing tomorrow.'

'What!' She stared at him aghast. 'Are you saying we are being deported?'

The ghost of a smile touched his lips. 'Nothing quite so dramatic as that.'

'I don't think Dee will be too happy — she arranged this holiday.'

'I know,' he replied quietly, 'and that brings me to the second condition.'

'Which is?' she raised her eyebrows, bracing herself for whatever was to follow.

'Dee,' he replied simply. 'She is to remain here.'

'I don't understand. I am to be sent home like a naughty schoolgirl and Dee is allowed to remain?' Justine's voice had risen and there was a spark of anger in her eyes as she stared defiantly at Cal.

He sighed and standing up began pacing the small room. 'No, Justine you've got it all wrong. You are being allowed to go home because I've managed to convince them you don't know anything, but where Dee's concerned it's another matter.'

Wildly she looked up at him. 'What are you saying?' When he remained silent she sprang to her feet and crossing the room caught at his arms forcing him to look at her. 'Cal, tell me what you mean.'

'Dee's been charged,' he replied.

'Charged? But what with?'

'Conspiracy.'

Slowly she dropped her hands and stepped back then without taking her eyes from Cal's, she said, 'This is all to do with Ramon, isn't it?'

'I wondered when you'd realise that.' Taking her hands he said gently, 'Look Justine, I think it's best if we go now, before they change their minds.'

'But how can I?' she cried, 'I can't leave Dee here on her own. In fact I won't!' she said stubbornly.

'You don't have any choice,' said

Cal grimly. 'Honestly Justine, it was as much as I could do to get them to let you go. But don't worry about leaving Dee, she's phoned her father and he's arriving tomorrow with the family lawyer who no doubt will get her off the hook.'

There was a cryptic note in his voice and Justine threw him a sharp look then narrowing her eyes, she said, 'You still haven't told me what she is supposed to have done . . . you said conspiracy but to what for heaven's sake?'

Cal sighed then taking a deep breath he said, 'Ramon Amador has been detained on drugs charges.'

Justine's eyes widened in dismay.

'He is believed to be a member of an international gang of drug dealers.'

'But Dee wouldn't have anything to do with it. Surely you don't believe that?' she cried.

He shrugged. 'It isn't for me to say what I think but your friend is going to have to prove she doesn't

194

have anything to do with Amador or his dubious activities.' As he finished speaking, the door suddenly opened revealing the man with the moustache. The policeman stood behind him and Justine noticed he wasn't grinning now.

The first man who was in plain clothes and who seemed to be in charge said something to Cal who answered him in Spanish. Then Cal turned to Justine. 'Are you ready?'

She looked from Cal to the man in the doorway then taking a deep breath she said, 'I'm not going anywhere until I've seen Dee.'

'Justine, will you please be reasonable,' growled Cal.

She sat down again on the bed, Cal glared angrily at her then he shrugged and turning to the man spoke in rapid Spanish.

The man frowned, muttered something, leaned forward to get a better look at Justine then turned on his heel and marched from the room.

'What did he say?' Justine was not

feeling as brave as she may have sounded.

'He said you can see her for five minutes only,' said Cal. He sounded kinder now, more like the Cal she had known before this nightmare; known and loved.

She stood up and together they followed the uniformed policeman down a corridor to a room identical to the one Justine had been in. He unlocked the door and as it swung open he stood back for them to enter then followed them into the room.

Dee was sitting at the table, she looked up sharply as they came in and Justine thought it looked as if she had been crying.

'Oh Dee,' she started forward and as Dee stood up they clasped each other.

'Justine, I'm sorry. I didn't mean to get you in this mess — you must believe me, I honestly didn't know . . . '

'Of course I believe you — everything will be all right when your father gets here . . . ' Justine was holding her friend by the shoulders then suddenly she paused and stared at her for there was a look of pure hatred on her face. 'What is it, Dee? What's the matter?' then as she turned she realised Dee was looking at Cal. Before she had the chance to say anything Dee's lip curled contemptuously.

'I don't know how you've got the nerve to show your face again,' she spat at Cal.

'Dee!' cried Justine in horror. 'You've got it all wrong. Cal's been marvellous. He's negotiated my release and he tried hard for yours but . . . '

'Like hell he did,' sneered Dee. 'Has he told you what he does for a living? Historical writer my foot, I had my doubts from the moment we met him . . . '

'Just a minute Dee, Cal has told me he's a policeman but you can hardly blame him for what's happened.'

'Can't I?' asked Dee doing nothing to keep the sarcasm from her voice.

'Well, when you're travelling cosily home with him tomorrow, ask him who tipped off the Spanish police this morning.'

Justine stared at her in bewilderment but before she had time to say anymore the policeman was gesturing that they had to leave.

'Oh, no please, not yet,' protested Justine wildly looking from Dee to Cal who were eyeing each other like two prize fighters. But her protest was in vain and she was ushered from the room managing only to shout goodbye to Dee and that she would see her soon back in England.

At last they stepped outside into the late afternoon sunshine and Justine stood for a moment taking several deep breaths then she felt Cal take her elbow and she allowed herself to be guided to his car. She collapsed into the passenger seat and as he drove away she realised she was trembling. Closing her eyes to fight the tears that threatened she leaned her head back in relief that she was free.

They drove out of the town in silence then when Justine opened her eyes she saw they were travelling through the orange groves. She glanced apprehensively at Cal but his expression was set as he concentrated on the road ahead.

'Cal,' she began tentatively, continuing only when he threw her a questioning glance, 'you must forgive Dee. She was over-wrought, I'm sure she didn't mean it.'

He gave a slight shrug. 'As you say, she was over-wrought,' he said as they turned into the road to Las Bellotas.

'Do you really think her father and their lawyer will be able to get her released?' she asked anxiously.

By this time they were climbing the hill and Cal shook his head, 'I don't know,' he replied. 'It depends what evidence the Spanish authorities have.'

'I can't see they have any,' said Justine. 'Honestly, Cal, Dee would be the last person to be involved in the drug scene. She hates drugs of any description, she won't even take an aspirin.'

'Most dealers are the same,' replied Cal evenly, 'it's the money they're interested in, not the product.'

Justine bit her lip realising how stupid she must have sounded then Cal drew into the drive of Casa Rafael, brought the car to a halt and leaning over, pulled her towards him and roughly kissed her. For a moment she struggled, trying to protest then she gave in and responded to his sudden sense of urgency.

Between kisses, he said, 'I know how you feel about Dee, and I'm sorry this has happened to spoil your holiday, but there is nothing you can do, so why don't we try and make the most of the few hours we have left?'

'But . . . ' Justine glanced towards the villa next door. 'Really I should pack . . . '

'Not now,' he murmured as he dropped light kisses on her forehead, her eyelids, the tip of her nose and finally her lips again, 'There'll be time enough for that later. Let's go inside.'

With a sigh she followed him, her excitement gathering like a tidal wave as they hurtled headlong towards the inevitable. Dozens of questions hovered in her mind, questions she knew sooner or later she would have to seek answers to. So many things didn't fit. The whole thing was like a giant jigsaw, some of the pieces were still missing and the ones she did have were muddled, but at that moment her brain was refusing to cope with any sort of puzzle, it was only responding to the urgent demands of her body.

As she followed Cal up the spiral staircase she was vaguely aware of the orchestration of the cicadas in the pines, the overpowering scent of flowering shrubs and the heat of the Spanish sun on her bare limbs. But today these sensations and delights were secondary, for her mind and every nerve in her body was focused on the man who was with her. She watched adoringly as he unlocked the door, loving every movement of his lithe body, the tanned limbs with their covering of dark gold hair, the sharp, hawk-like profile and the thick mass of tawny hair that flowed back from the widow's peak. If had come as a surprise to learn that he was a policeman and not a writer but at that moment Justine was incapable of questioning his deception. She only knew she wouldn't have cared what he was. She loved him and she wanted him with a depth of desire she'd never known before.

The door swung open and they walked into the lounge then he turned and took her hand and the look in his eyes told her all she wanted to know; his desire matched hers and this time nothing would be allowed to interrupt their lovemaking. His fingers closed around hers, cool and strong and she shivered with anticipation, then gently but firmly he drew her towards a room, which she knew instinctively would be the bedroom.

It was a beautiful room obviously the master bedroom of the Casa Rafael, soft and cool in shades of magnolia, cinnamon and dusky pink, its furniture the richest shade of mahogany and the king sized bed covered with pink satin sheets.

'Oh Cal,' she whispered, 'it's beautiful.'

'Nothing could be too good for you,' he replied, his voice sexily husky as he stood back and looked at her, his eyes adoring her figure clad only in shorts and suntop and her long dark hair tumbling over her tanned shoulders. 'You know, Justine, you really are lovely . . .' his breath caught in his throat and as he took a step forward, Justine put a hand to her hair as if suddenly conscious of the way she must look.

'I really should take a shower,' she began, then she was silenced as her drew her hungrily into his arms and brought his lips down on hers.

'Maybe you should,' he murmured after a while, 'maybe I should. Maybe we will . . . but not yet because I want you, Justine, I want you now, and this time nothing will prevent us.' He unfastened the tiny buttons on her suntop which he then slipped over her arms letting it drop onto the thick carpet. She wasn't wearing a bra and he caught his breath at the sight of her breasts, then dropping to his knees he grasped her hips and drew her towards him. As he undid the fastening on her shorts he kissed the smooth skin of her stomach letting his tongue gently tease her navel.

Justine shuddered with delight, the blood in her veins like liquid fire as she lifted her head in abandon arching her back as he eased her shorts then her briefs to the ground drawing her towards him with a sudden groan of desire. Moments later he had discarded his own clothes and had carried her to the bed then lowering himself above her he caught her hands imprisoning them above her head as his mouth once again sought hers.

Hungrily she responded, returning his kisses with a fervency which amazed and delighted him while straining her body towards his so that their naked flesh touched at every conceivable point. Gently, expertly he aroused her even further taking her to the very brink of unimagined pleasure as with hands and lips he caressed, teased and moulded the soft silky skin of her body leaving her aching with unfulfilled desire.

When he finally parted her thighs the moment of penetration was so exquisite that she cried out in delight and gave herself to him in total surrender.

Never had Justine known such sweetness and as Cal moved, unable to hold back any longer, the intensity of her pleasure was matched only by the perfection of the moment of fulfilment.

Later when they lay in each other's arms in a tangle of pink satin with Cal curling strands of her hair around his fingers, Justine propped herself on her elbow and looked down at him.

'Cal?'

'Mmm?' he murmured drowsily.

'Did you offer to escort me back to England?'

'What do you think?' He grinned up at her.

'I know you said you're not really on holiday but won't it interfere with your plans?'

'Not really, it's all part of the job.'

She frowned. 'You were involved then in this business with Ramon?'

He hesitated. 'Yes,' he admitted at last, 'you could say that . . . but let's not talk about that now. You know you said earlier you'd like a shower? Well, I have a better idea, how about a dip in the pool?'

She giggled. 'You mean skinny-dipping?'

'What else?' He rolled over and out of bed, then taking her hand he pulled her up and they ran together out of the bedroom, down the staircase and across the *naya* to the pool. The water was deep and deliciously cool and Justine gasped with the sudden shock as she surfaced and shook the water from her eyes.

For a moment she couldn't see Cal, then from behind she felt his arms go round her, felt his hard lean body pressed against hers, then her breasts were cupped in his hands. She leaned against him as a thrill of desire shot through her and he buried his face against her throat, his wild kisses driving her frantic again with longing. Then turning her to face him, he pulled her fiercely towards him and for the second time he made love to her right there in the pool with the late afternoon sun sparkling on the water and the scent of jasmine enveloping them. And it was this time that as he held her face cupped in his hands and stared down deeply into her eyes, he told her he loved her.

'God help me, Justine, I never meant

it to happen, but it has.'

Laughing up at him she kissed the tips of her fingers and gently placed them on his lips. 'I love you too, Cal,' she said softly. 'And I wasn't looking for love either but when it happens there's little you can do about it.' As she spoke she thought about Dee and how she loved Ramon and she felt a stab of guilt that she should be here so happy with Cal when her friend was languishing in a Spanish gaol but as Cal had said, there was nothing more she could do, so she might as well enjoy the time they had together. At the back of her mind there still niggled the thought that Cal had said he would be bound to hurt her, but she tried to dismiss that also and concentrate on the sheer heaven of the moment.

Later they took the promised shower, laughing and loving and soaping each other. Then at last when they were both dry and wrapped in towelling robes, Cal poured glasses of chilled white wine and they sat together on the *naya* and watched the sun disappear behind the distant hills.

This has been the most incredible day of my life, thought Justine as she rested her head on Cal's shoulder, not only have I been more frightened but I've also been happier than ever before.

Cal prepared dinner; steak and salad, then after they'd eaten and he'd made love to her again they slept in each other's arms for a few hours before he gently woke her and told her she would have to go and pack if they were to get to Alicante for their flight. It was still dark when they left Casa Rafael. Stars dotted the vast expanse of sky and for once all was silent, even the cicadas, and the dogs in the valley.

Justine opened the front door of the villa while Cal stood on the *naya* leaning against the balcony. She glanced over her shoulder and smiled before flicking on the light switch. At first all seemed normal but as Justine glanced around the lounge she suddenly frowned.

'What's been going on in here?' she said slowly as she walked into the room.

By this time Cal had followed her. 'What's wrong, Justine?'

'I'm not sure.' She shook her head. 'Just a minute . . . ' she hurried from the room. In her bedroom she switched on the light then swiftly scanned the room.

As Cal joined her she said, 'Someone's been in here, Cal. Things have been moved. That scarf was on the bed, it's on the chair now.' She pulled open one of the drawers, 'And look, here, someone has been through my clothes, I know they have . . . Cal . . . ?' her voice rose on a note of hysteria then she was conscious of his arms closing around her.

She thought he was going to tell her she was imagining things, that no one else had been in the villa, but to her astonishment, he said, 'Justine, please, listen to me. You are right, the villa has been searched.'

'Why?' she stared at him blankly.

'It had to be after you and Dee were arrested. They had to be sure there weren't any drugs here.'

'I see . . . ' Slowly she pulled away from him and sank down onto the bed. For a long moment she sat still, a puzzled expression on her face then looking up at Cal she said slowly, 'Cal, how did you know about this?'

He had crossed to the window and was fiddling with the catch and didn't answer immediately.

Justine watched him then rose to her feet. 'Cal, I have to know, please answer me.'

With a sigh he turned to face her. 'I know about it Justine, because I made the search.'

11

'Why would you search our belongings?' Justine stared at him in bewilderment.

He carried on examining the window catch then without looking at her, he said, 'Someone had to do it, Justine and I thought you would rather it was me than a Spanish policeman.' He glanced at her and she thought she detected embarrassment in his look.

'Yes,' she admitted at last. 'I am glad it was you but I'm not sure why it was necessary. In fact there is a great deal I don't understand . . . '

'I'm sure there is,' said Cal. He hesitated then carefully he said, 'I'm to blame, Justine, I should never have allowed things to have gone so far between us.'

She stared at him hardly able to believe what she was hearing after the night they had just spent. 'Are you saying you regret what we've done?' she whispered as her world began to fall apart.

'No!' he retorted, then his shoulders sagged. 'Of course I don't regret it, how could I? But nothing can alter the fact that you were in my care and I shouldn't have allowed my feelings to get the better of me.' They stared at each other in agonised silence then at last he said, 'We have very little time if we're to catch that flight.' He glanced at his watch. 'How quickly can you be ready?'

'I need to change, but it won't take me long to pack,' she replied woodenly.

He nodded. 'I'll get my gear then bring the car round.' He walked to the door then paused as Justine spoke again.

'What should I do about Dee's things?'

'Leave them, you can't take them with you. Her father will sort everything out.'

As he left the room Justine stared after him in dismay. It seemed as if the magical time they had shared was over and Cal was now very much an on-duty policeman. He had as good as admitted what had happened between them had been a mistake, although she could have sworn he had felt the same way as she had. Hurriedly she changed into jeans and a sweatshirt and tied her hair back then she began throwing her clothes into her case. When she was ready Cal stowed her case and his holdall into the boot of the Renault while she made a last check round the villa to make sure all was secure.

Dawn was breaking as they drove away and Justine threw one last regretful glance over her shoulder wishing that things had turned out differently and that she could stay. She had come to love Las Bellotas; the beauty of the countryside, the hot Spanish sun, the ancient buildings steeped in history and the passionate people and she hoped desperately one day she would be able to return.

The first pearly light lit the sky as they drove through the deserted orange groves, ghostly now in the strange half light.

Justine stole a glance at Cal but when she saw his set profile she decided to remain silent. The anguish deep inside persisted however and she dreaded hearing answers to the questions she knew had to be asked. She wanted nothing to destroy her happiness for the time she had spent with Cal had been like nothing she had ever experienced before. She knew she loved him with all her heart and while she had come to hope he might feel the same way, many doubts now niggled at the back of her mind.

They left Javea joining the southbound motorway for Alicante and for the greater part of the journey they remained silent as Cal put his foot down in a determined effort to be in time for their flight.

When they drew into the carpark

from where Cal's hired Renault would later be picked up, he glanced at his watch and gave a sigh of relief. He had completed the journey with time to spare. Their strange subdued mood persisted as they checked in, then sat in the airport lounge and drank coffee. Justine longed to break the tension, to ask the questions she could avoid no longer, to accept his answers, then for everything to be as it had the night before. But the fact that he had searched her belongings and not told her had heralded a change in their relationship, followed by his confession that he should never have allowed himself to make love to her. After that the tension had magnified as she waited for the right moment to ask for explanations.

It came shortly after take-off as the aircraft headed up the coast before turning inland for its journey across Spain and France. From her seat by the window Justine suddenly saw Montgo far below and she leaned forward for a better view. And there it all was spread out below her, sparkling in the early morning sunlight; the bright blue of the Mediterranean, Montgo guarding the old town, the port with its rows of boats, the dark masses of the orange groves and the paler strip of sandy beach.

'Look,' Justine moved back so that Cal could see, 'it's Javea . . . there's Montgo . . . and you can even see Las Bellotas in that mass of trees on the hills.' Her voice wavered as she thought of Dee locked up in that awful room and how different this was from the moment they had landed. They had been so excited about their holiday, now it was over, cut short in the most distressing way.

As if he read her thoughts Cal took her hand and squeezed it. 'So it's goodbye to Javea,' he murmured looking down at the scene below, then as the plane banked sharply, turning inland he sat back in his seat.

'What I don't understand is why

you were there in the first place,' said Justine slowly. She felt him grow very still and hardly dared to look at him. 'You've told me you weren't on holiday and that you are a policeman. I must admit I'm not too surprised to learn that you're not a writer, at least not a historian.'

He gave a rueful smile. 'Was it that obvious?'

'It became so, you may have got away with it until the fiesta in Altea because until then I thought you were just shaky on British history. When I realised you didn't know much Spanish history either, I began to wonder how you were managing to write a book on it.'

'It was just my luck to pick a cover like that, then to meet an authority on the subject.'

'I'd hardly call myself an authority . . .'

'You knew a darn sight more than I did!' They both laughed and it helped to ease the tension.

Then Justine grew serious again

determined now to find out what she wanted to know. 'So, you're not a writer, you are a policeman and you are not even an off-duty policeman enjoying a break in the Spanish sun.'

'True, but one fact I must put you straight on is that I am actually a detective and I'm with the Drug Squad.'

She raised her eyebrows. 'Hence the connection between Ramon Amador and the drug charges?' When he nodded she asked curiously, 'Did you know about Ramon before you came to Spain? Were you following him?'

'I wasn't so much following him as trying to find him.' He gave a long pause then glancing uneasily at Justine he said, 'In actual fact it was Dee I was following, in the assumption that she would lead me to him. And in the end of course, she did just that.'

She stared at him in amazement. 'But why should you think Dee would lead you to him? How did you know she knew him? Even I didn't know that until we got to Spain.'

'Justine,' he said gently, 'Dee has been under surveillance for some time.'

She looked shocked then she frowned. 'But why? I don't understand . . . I refuse to believe she's involved in anything like that . . . '

'If that's the case she shouldn't mix with the likes of Amador,' he commented drily. 'She came under suspicion during Cowes week when she was constantly seen with him. Shortly after that he gave us the slip and I was assigned to watch Dee for we felt sure that sooner or later she would be in contact with him. Amador's a nasty piece of work, he's wanted in several countries on drug dealing charges, but he's also been known to work in the company of beautiful women.'

'But how did you know Dee . . . we . . . were going to Javea?'

'I told you we were keeping a close watch on Dee, there was very little she did that we didn't know about. We knew the flight she'd booked and about the villa, Las Bellotas then we realised she'd booked two tickets. At first we thought the second ticket was for Amador and we thought we had him, that he'd simply been in hiding and was going to meet her at the airport. Then you appeared and that threw us because we didn't know who you were. You hadn't met Dee during the time we had been watching her and we weren't sure how closely involved you were.'

'We hadn't seen each other for some time,' admitted Justine, 'but surely Cal, if Dee had been involved in any shady business, she'd have hardly taken me along. I'd have simply got in the way.'

He shrugged. 'Maybe, but we didn't know whether you were involved as well, or on the other hand, you could have simply been her cover.'

Justine frowned, biting her lip, then glancing sharply at Cal she said, 'But how did you come to be staying next door? Don't tell me that was a coincidence?'

'Of course it wasn't. When we found out where you were heading, my office made inquiries about the other properties near Las Bellotas and found that the owners of Casa Rafael were in Australia, so by liaising with the Spanish authorities they arranged for me to be 'staying' there when you arrived. I understand the owners were only too pleased to have a detective guarding their property while they were away.'

Justine stared at him incredulously. 'So how long had you been there when we arrived?'

'I'd only got there the day before,' he confessed.

'That's why you weren't very tanned,' said Justine.

'I'm beginning to think you should have been a detective,' replied Cal ruefully.

The Spanish stewardess appeared with the refreshment trolley and Justine realised they hadn't had any breakfast. Although she didn't feel hungry she forced herself to eat. She was feeling shocked and bewildered by all that Cal had told her but there were still things that puzzled her.

'You saw me that day in the church, didn't you?' Cal asked a little later.

She nodded. 'I thought it was you, but when you didn't mention it, I wondered if I'd been mistaken.'

'I thought you were Dee,' he said simply.

'But why should you think that?'

'You split up that day didn't you?'

'Yes,' she said slowly. 'Dee went to the beach and I wanted to see that church.' Then suddenly she remembered. 'We changed tops didn't we?'

He nodded. 'You did and confused me completely. I ended up following who I thought was Dee in her red suntop and it turned out to be you. To confuse matters further you were both wearing those sunhats and you'd tucked your hair inside yours. I was convinced I was on to something when you split up, I thought Dee had arranged to meet Amador in that church, then I realised it was you and I thought you had tricked me.'

'Me?' asked Justine in surprise.

'Either you, Dee, or both of you. I wasn't sure what to think.'

Justine frowned. 'Earlier you said about following Dee during Cowes week, so she was right when she said she had seen you there?'

He nodded, 'It must have been one night when she left her uncle's yacht with Amador. She seemed so wrapped up in him I didn't dream she'd noticed me. We suspected he thought the yacht was Dee's and that he was trying to persuade her to let him use it for one of his drug running trips.'

Justine was silent for a moment as she remembered what Dee had told her about the nights she had spent with her Spanish lover aboard her uncle's yacht. Then she turned to Cal again, 'So you lied when you said you hadn't visited the Isle of Wight since you were a boy?'

'I'm afraid I did.' He smiled apologetically. 'I had to Justine, I didn't want anything to connect me with Cowes week or Amador. It came as a shock when you told me yesterday morning that Dee had remembered seeing me there. I feared my cover was blown, I had to act fast.'

'What do you mean?' She turned and looked at him. All of a sudden he looked exhausted and her heart went out to him but her nerves were on edge as she waited for his reply.

'When she got back from Altea, Dee said she was meeting Amador on that yacht the next morning, then when you told me that she had remembered where she had seen me, I was afraid she would tell him, so I knew the time had come to round things up.' He paused then with a nod of satisfaction he added, 'The fact that we also got two other members of the same gang was a sheer bonus.'

Justine took a deep breath. 'So it

was you who tipped off the Spanish police?'

'I thought you realised that,' he said gently.

'Dee was right all along . . . and I wouldn't believe her,' said Justine slowly. 'I even went on at her for being so rude to you.'

'Justine, please,' he took hold of her hand, 'listen, I had no choice, believe me.'

'My God, what a naïve fool I've been,' she cried snatching her hand away. 'What a laugh you must have had at my expense.'

'Of course I haven't,' he protested. 'You mustn't think that. It simply had to be done.'

'But surely you don't think Dee is involved,' she cried. 'Not in something so evil as that!' When he didn't reply she went on in the same anguished tone, 'You can't think that, Cal, you just can't!'

'But she is involved with Amador,' he said softly.

'That's simply because she loves him, it's nothing to do with anything else. I'll stake my life on it. I know her, Cal, — you don't.'

One or two of the other passengers had become aware of the argument and were glancing in their direction and Cal began to look uncomfortable. He stirred restlessly in his seat. 'Justine, please,' he murmured glancing over his shoulder, 'please try and calm down.'

'I am calm,' she snapped and glared angrily out of the window.

'You have to admit,' he said after a moment, 'it did look suspicious, especially in Altea when she waited until the one moment I was preoccupied to give me the slip.'

'She explained that,' retorted Justine.

'I know, but there was no getting away from the fact that was the moment she made contact with Amador.'

Justine gave an angry sigh. 'I still don't understand what Dee is supposed to have done, you said conspiracy but to what, for God's sake?' Her voice had risen again and Cal glanced round.

'Justine, please keep your voice down, I'm not even supposed to be discussing this with you.'

'Then why are you?' she retorted.

He was silent and she turned and as her eyes met his he sighed. 'Because I care about you.'

They stared helplessly at each other reliving the passion they had so recently shared then Justine felt the tears pricking the back of her eyes and she was forced to look away.

They were silent after that. Cal, grim and weary from exhaustion and Justine so keyed up with emotion that she hardly trusted herself to speak. When they landed at Heathrow they were met by two plain clothes detectives who escorted Justine through Customs where her belongings were subjected to a thorough search. Then she was told she could go home but that she must be prepared to answer questions if the need arose.

'Will you go straight back to the Isle

of Wight?' asked Cal as he helped her with her luggage.

She nodded wearily. 'Yes, I can get a boat-train to Portsmouth Harbour from Waterloo.'

'I'll get a taxi and come to Waterloo with you, then I have to report to my office.'

She didn't have the strength to argue with him but it wasn't until they were seated in the back of the London cab that it suddenly occurred to her that she might never see Cal again, that this brief journey could be the last moments they would spend together. Wildly she looked at him but his face was turned away as he stared at the rainwashed streets.

She took a deep breath, 'Cal, I know you said you shouldn't discuss it but please will you tell me something?'

He turned towards her and her heart jolted painfully at the look in his eyes. She swallowed, 'Do you seriously believe Dee is guilty?'

He sighed and shrugged. 'I thought

so at first . . . but now . . . I don't know. You've put doubts in my mind, Justine. But it doesn't make any difference what I think, it's out of my hands.'

When the taxi arrived at Waterloo, Cal told her to get her ticket while he paid the driver and sorted out her luggage. She returned from the ticket office to find him waiting by the bookshop. He was wearing a brown leather jacket with his denims and looked achingly handsome. He didn't hear her approach as he was scanning a newspaper, so for a brief instant she was able to watch him unobserved, then as he looked up the moment was gone. The sadness was back in his eyes and she tried to swallow the lump in her throat.

'Have you got your ticket?'

'Yes,' she whispered.

'What time is your train?'

'It leaves in a few minutes.'

He bent down and picked up her case.

'Won't you need a platform ticket?' she asked as they approached the barrier.

He shook his head and she saw he was carrying his identification card and her heart thudded painfully as she realised that this was no fond farewell, but Cal simply carrying out his duties to the bitter end. She boarded the train with Cal behind her and by the time he had stowed her luggage on the rack the guard was already checking the doors. Cal leapt out onto the platform and Justine wound down the window. He stared up at her then stepping forward he gripped her hand. 'Justine . . . I . . . ' he began.

'Cal, tell me one thing,' she said and her words came out in a rush. 'Did you ever believe I was involved?'

He stared at her, then as the whistle sounded he said, 'I thought you might have been, but as I got to know you, I knew you weren't.'

'Was that the only reason you got to know me, to prove something?' Her eyes were full of tears now. 'Was that all it was, Cal?' Wildly she looked down at him and saw the anguish in his own eyes.

'Of course it wasn't . . . '

The train had begun to move, still he held her hand then desperately as he released her, he shouted, 'When this is all over . . . the investigation . . . I'll . . . ' but his words were lost as the train rapidly gathered speed. Justine leaned out of the window and her last glimpse of him was as he raised his hand, then as the train rounded a bend in the track, he was gone.

Fighting the tears which were already trickling down her cheeks she sank into her seat oblivious of the other passengers in the compartment as the train took her away from the man whom only a short week ago had been a stranger, a man she had come to love with all her heart only to find that he had used her.

12

The cross-Solent ferry trip to the Isle of Wight was choppy, the weather wet and blustery but Justine hardly noticed for all she could think of was getting home and shutting the door on the pain and heartache.

The small whitewashed cottage where she lived with her mother was one of a terrace in the village of Seaview. The long narrow gardens ran right down to the beach and when Justine arrived in the taxi that had brought her from the station it was to find the cottage empty. Her mother was visiting her sister in Bournemouth and Justine decided not to contact her as she would only worry about what had happened and would want to cut short her own holiday and come home. Much as Justine loved her mother she now felt an overwhelming need for solitude. She wasn't due back at her job at Osborne House for another week so she had time to try and come to terms with what had happened.

For the next few days the weather remained squally and she rarely left the cottage but towards the end of the week as the weather improved she began to take long solitary walks along the beach.

Since arriving home Justine doubted that Cal had been out of her thoughts for more than a few seconds. Every waking moment he was there, his image strong and clear in her mind, the sound of his voice in her head and when she closed her eyes she could imagine the feel of him beneath her hands, the pressure of his body against hers and the taste of his kisses.

At night when sleep finally claimed her, her dreams were filled with him, precious images that dissolved with the dawn when she remembered that he'd gone.

And throughout it all the agony remained; he had used her. Gradually, during her walks beside the Solent, she came to understand what he had meant when he had said that he would be bound to hurt her. At the time she had innocently imagined he meant she would be hurt because he was involved elsewhere and she had almost accepted that, but the reality had been more cruel. He had used her and the pain that came with the realisation of that was almost more than she could bear.

The more she had thought about what had happened and gone over Cal's explanations, the more convinced she became that he had recognised she was attracted to him from the moment they had met. He had then gone on to use that fact to enable him to acquire the information he needed and to be able to follow Dee. As if all that hadn't been enough, he had used her further by taking advantage of the situation and making love to her after Dee and Ramon had been arrested, later adding insult to injury by telling her he should never have allowed it to happen.

Together with her torment over Cal was the worry about Dee and what was happening to her in Spain. She had tried phoning her home on several occasions but there was never any reply and she hesitated over phoning Dee's office as she wasn't sure whether they knew what had happened.

As the days slowly passed, each more agonising than the one before, Justine wondered if she would ever get over Cal, then one morning she awoke to find the sun shining. She lay for a long time staring at the ceiling then she realised that for the first time anger had crept in to replace some of the pain she had felt, anger with Cal for what he had done but more important, anger with herself for allowing herself to be taken in.

This anger seemed to galvanise her into action and feeling more positive she set off after breakfast to the shops in the village to stock up with some food before her mother's expected return in a few days' time.

It was while she was packing the groceries away in the kitchen that the doorbell suddenly rang. She paused and frowned. No one knew she was home yet, so she certainly wasn't expecting anyone and she certainly didn't feel like entertaining. Slowly she walked through to the hall and opened the front door, then her eyes widened in amazement.

Dee was standing on the doorstep.

For a moment they simply stared at each other then they fell into each other's arms.

'Oh, Dee, thank God you're home,' Justine cried hugging her tightly.

'You can say that again,' replied Dee and her voice had a husky note to it. 'But aren't you going to ask me in?'

'Of course I am,' said Justine and glancing past Dee she saw her friend's red sports car parked by the gate. She stood back and Dee stepped into the hall then as she closed the door Dee followed her into the tiny livingroom.

'Let's sit in the conservatory,' said Justine. 'I must know what's been happening. I've been so worried about you but I didn't know who to contact as I didn't know who knew what.'

They sat down on the comfortable old garden chairs in the sunny conservatory at the rear of the cottage and as Justine anxiously studied her friend's face she noticed her drawn expression and the lines of fatigue. 'When did you get back?' she asked, her own pain forgotten in her concern for Dee.

'Yesterday,' Dee replied. 'Believe me, I've done some travelling in my time, but I've never in my life been more pleased to see dear old Heathrow.'

'So what happened?' Justine leaned forward anxiously. 'What about the charges?'

'Dropped, all of them,' said Dee almost flippantly then seeing Justine's expression she added, 'Insufficient evidence apparently. They had nothing to hold me on. Our lawyer soon sorted it out.' She stretched out her hand and began examining her nails.

Justine stared at her then slowly she

asked, 'And Ramon?'

Dee didn't answer immediately, continuing to admire her nails as if that were the most important issue in the world, then when Justine remained silent, she glanced up and Justine saw the glint of unshed tears in her eyes.

'Dee . . . I, that is if you'd rather not . . . '

'No, it's OK, you might as well know now,' she took a deep breath, 'Ramon will be going to gaol for a very long time.'

'Oh, Dee, I am sorry.'

'What?' Dee looked up quickly, an expression of false brightness on her face, 'Oh, don't be sorry . . . he had it coming to him — and for a long time apparently . . . ' she swallowed and trailed off, unable to continue.

Justine slid from her chair and kneeling beside Dee put her arms round her allowing her to sob unashamedly for some considerable time.

When she had recovered a little, Justine said, 'I'm sorry, Dee, really I am, I know how much you love him.'

Dee looked up, then blowing her nose hard, she said, 'Would you mind re-phrasing that please and using the past tense?'

'What do you mean?' Justine frowned.

'You said you know how much I love him, I would prefer that to be, how much I loved him.'

'You mean you . . . ?'

'Don't love him now? Too right I don't,' she said grimly. 'I couldn't love a rat like that, Jus. Drug traders are the scum of the earth as far as I'm concerned. And to think he tried to involve me in his beastly activities.'

'He did?' Justine raised her eyebrows. 'I wasn't sure. I didn't know whether he actually tried to do so or whether the police only suspected that he had.'

'It was when he was here on the island during Cowes week, I didn't realise it at the time — but when I was in that rotten cell, I had lots of time to think — and I remembered that the exact time he seemed to lose interest in me was the night he discovered that my uncle's yacht didn't belong to me. Apparently he thought he could persuade me to let him use it or even help him to use it for his dirty deeds. When he found out it wasn't mine, he disappeared, obviously never expecting to see or hear from me again, which of course he wouldn't have done if I hadn't gone chasing off to Javea after him, dragging you with me. My God, the crazy things we do when we think we're in love. You even tried to warn me, didn't you, Jus? But would I listen?' She shook her head raising her eyes suggesting that she was a hopeless case, then suddenly she paused, looking searchingly at Justine as if she had just become aware that her friend had grown very quiet.

'Justine . . . ' she hesitated. 'What about you?'

'What about me?' Justine slowly turned her head and Dee couldn't have failed to see the pain in her eyes.

'Oh my God,' she said leaning

forward and taking Justine's hand, 'here's me rabbiting on and there's you quite obviously suffering every bit, if not more, than me. What is it, Jus?' Her voice was soft now, gentle as she probed for the truth.

Justine shook her head not able for a moment to trust her voice.

'It's him, isn't it, it's that copper?'

Justine was forced to smile at that, then biting her lip she said, 'Actually he's a detective.'

'I don't care what he damn well is.' Dee exploded. 'He spied on us, he bloody well got me arrested then left me to rot in a Spanish hell hole!'

'I know,' whispered Justine.

'He probably even tricked you into going to bed with him, didn't he?' demanded Dee, then added, 'you needn't bother to answer, I can see I was right from the look on your face.' She stood up and began pacing the minute floor space of the conservatory. 'He's another rat, you know, Jus,' she turned to Justine to emphasise the point.

'I know,' Justine sniffed and nodded.

'In fact, I'd go so far to say that he's as bad as Ramon,' she paused in her tirade and glanced sharply at Justine, then seeing the look on her face she said, 'Well, no perhaps not quite so bad, but bad enough and certainly not worth bothering about or losing any sleep over.' She fell silent, stopped pacing the floor and sat down again, then throwing Justine a shrewd glance she said, 'Was he good? In bed I mean?'

'Dee!' protested Justine.

'Sorry,' Dee held up her hands, 'but it's so unusual for you to get that smitten over anyone that I figure he must have something. To tell the truth I was getting a bit worried about you . . . you seemed so fussy over men. But it looks as if you've picked a non-starter with him, doesn't it?' She peered at Justine then she said, 'You're in love with him, aren't you?'

Justine shrugged. 'I'm angry with

him,' she said. 'I'm angry because he used me. He used me to get to you, then he took advantage of the situation.'

Dee continued to stare thoughtfully at her then glancing at her watch she stood up again saying, 'Well, Jus, I have to go. I only dropped by to see if you were OK and to tell you what had happened. I'm sorry about all this, you know, and that your holiday was ruined. I promise I'll try and make it up to you sometime.'

After Dee had gone Justine reflected on what she had told her and eventually came to the conclusion that she would just have to try and forget Cal and get over him in the same way that Dee appeared to have done over Ramon. But somehow she doubted it would be that easy. She'd never fallen so hard for anyone as she had for Cal Douglas and she had a feeling that he wouldn't be that easy to forget.

The following day also turned out to be warm and sunny and in the afternoon after Justine had cleaned the house she went to sit in the conservatory to make the most of the September sunshine. It proved however to be hotter than she thought and after a while she carried her chair into the garden and placed it beneath a chestnut tree in the shelter of the old stone wall that separated the garden from the beach.

From where she was sitting she had a clear view of the shipping in the Solent and the mainland in the distance. The sea like the sky was a deep cobalt blue while the leaves of the tree above her were tipped with gold. The only sounds were the gentle swish of the waves on the shingle and a flock of gulls which swooped and screamed on dark patches of seaweed on the beach. Lifting her face to the sun she closed her eyes.

Although she still yearned for Cal, since talking to Dee the previous day, her anger had abated and she recognised it for the negative force it was. If Dee was able to accept what had happened to her and be prepared to forget Ramon then she too should try to get over what had happened.

She grew drowsy in the unexpected heat and after a while she imagined she was back at Las Bellotas. The cries of the gulls became the singing of cicadas and the late-summer smell of an English garden was replaced by the heady scent of jasmine and bougainvillaea.

Even the sun grew hotter and suddenly instead of the sea before her there was the sparkling blue of a swimming pool. Somewhere in the distance she heard the click of a garden gate but she ignored it, wanting to remain in that other dream world where love would be waiting for her. And sure enough even as she waited, willing him to appear, he was there beside her, his tall figure bronzed by the sun, his tawny mane of hair, and his curious golden eyes smiling down at her. He reached out his hand, and then she was in his arms, drowning in his embrace.

But even as it was happening she knew it was only a dream and with a sob she opened her eyes.

She didn't know how long she'd been asleep. The sun was still warm but it had moved and was casting longer shadows across the garden. The gulls were silent now but a tug off Spithead was sounding its hooter.

But something else had changed and Justine was uncertain what it was. Then very slowly she turned her head.

He was sitting on the grass, his back against the trunk of the old chestnut tree, watching her and although her pulses raced at the sight of him, she wasn't surprised to find him there. Her dream had been so real and it now seemed the most natural thing in the world that he should be there beside her.

Their eyes met and for a long time their gaze remained locked and there was no need for explanations. Then he rose slowly and looking down at her as he had in her dream he held out his hand and helped her to her feet.

For a while they stood beneath the old tree and simply looked at each other then gently Cal drew her towards him cupping her face in his hands allowing his fingers to become entangled in her hair. In that instant her pain and anger were forgotten because quite simply he had come back for her.

They made love in Justine's bedroom, a small white room full of country prints and dried flowers, a far cry from the elegance of the mahogany fittings and pink satin sheets of the Casa Rafael, but it didn't matter, for they were together.

And this time there was no long sensuous arousal while Cal undressed her, this time they were in a frenzy of desire, their clothes discarded in a trail on the floor, Justine's need as intense as Cal's.

She stretched out beneath him on the bed her eyes adoring the strong lines of his tanned, naked body then she opened her arms and their bodies melted together as if they had been making love for a lifetime.

The precious moment of possession had the satisfaction felt at the end of a long search. Then Justine gave herself up to the sheer magic she remembered from the last time, magic she had despaired of ever knowing again.

Later they lay satiated in each other's arms, their hair and bodies damp from exertion their senses at peace. Justine stirred and was about to ask Cal how he had found her but he, anticipating her questions rolled over and staring down at her put his fingers on her lips.

'Before you say anything, I want to get something absolutely straight,' he said.

She raised her eyebrows and stared up into his eyes. 'And what's that?'

'Simply that I love you,' he replied firmly lowering his head and planting a long demanding kiss on her parted lips, then raising his head again he went on, 'Now we have that settled,

I would imagine you've got plenty of questions for me.'

She smiled. 'Would you believe me if I said no?'

He shook his head and she laughed. 'No, I suppose you wouldn't, I did have questions, but they don't matter anymore. Especially after what you've just told me.'

'That I love you?' He smiled down at her and she felt her heart leap. 'It's true and I knew it from the moment I met you. But since then I've given you plenty of reason to doubt it. I'm sorry, Justine. I wouldn't have hurt you for the world.' He sighed then and rolled on to his back while she propped herself on her elbow and watched him.

'It was the wretched investigation,' he said at last. 'I had to put in a full report about what had happened and I didn't dare contact you until I'd cleared things with my chief. As it was I broke every rule in the book and a few that weren't. The trouble was I don't remember any rules that tell you what to do when you fall in love with a suspect, or as it turned out with the friend of a suspect.'

'And there was me thinking you had only used me to get to Dee,' said Justine slowly.

'And what about after Dee had been arrested?'

She felt the hot colour flood her face at the memory of the night they'd shared at the Casa Rafael. 'I thought you were just taking advantage of the situation.'

He stared at her then he groaned. 'Oh Justine, if only you knew, by then I loved you and wanted you so much that I don't think any force on earth could have stopped me. It was only in the cold light of day that I realised what I had done. In my bungling attempt to explain, I knew I had hurt you, I knew you thought I had used you and I went through hell waiting to get here to put things right.'

'Did you know that Dee is home?'

she asked after a while.

He nodded. 'Yes, the Spanish authorities have apparently dropped all charges against her. And in spite of what you might think, I'm glad. I hated to think of Dee mixed up with a character like Amador.'

'It just shows how you can be taken in when you're in love,' mused Justine. 'I think she'll get over it though. She came to see me yesterday,' she added smiling down at him as he began tracing patterns down her throat and across her shoulders with his fingertips.

'I know,' he said softly reaching up and kissing her again.

'You knew, but how?' she looked bewildered.

'She phoned me last night — at work would you believe? But then Dee never did anything by halves did she?'

'But why should she phone you?'

He took a deep breath. 'To tear me off a strip for the way I'd treated you.'

'She did what!' Justine sat up and

stared down at him in horror.

He gave a deep chuckle. 'She told me exactly what she thought of me. She even said she'd told you you were mad for falling in love with such a dubious character as me, then she laid into me for ruining the holiday, saying that it was bad enough that I'd got her wrongfully arrested but she was damned if she was going to let me get away with upsetting you.'

'Good grief, what did you say?' Justine pushed back her mass of dark hair unable to believe what she was hearing.

'I agreed with her. That took the wind out of her sails for a bit, then when I could get a word in, I told her that I was only waiting for my chief to clear my report then I'd be on the next ferry to the Isle of Wight. She said something about it being not before time then she hung up. You know something, my love, your friend Dee is quite a character.'

'She certainly is,' admitted Justine

helpless with laughter. 'She promised she would try and make things up to me but I never dreamt she would contact you.'

'As it turned out, I was on my way anyway but it was good of her to try and make amends. Do you think she'll get over Amador?'

Justine considered for a moment then she nodded slowly, 'I think so, her love has turned to hate for what he was and what he tried to make her do but . . . ' she paused and looked at him shyly.

'What is it,' he asked softly. 'What were you going to say?'

'Only that I'm glad I'm not being asked to get over you, because I don't think I ever could.'

'Good,' he said reaching out and pulling her on top of him so that she sat astride him. 'Because I don't want you ever to stop loving me, not for one minute and if you do I shall remind you again and again just how good it is between us.'

She leaned forward her hair falling

like a curtain around them, brushing his chest and as he lifted his head to kiss her he covered her breasts with his hands. His body stirred beneath her and she knew he was ready for her again.

★ ★ ★

Later as they strolled together hand in hand through the gently breaking surf Cal asked her to marry him.

'I'm not a historian, or even a writer,' he said pulling a face. 'Do you think you could bear to be the wife of a detective?'

Justine frowned pretending to consider.

Cal lifted her up into his arms and laughing up at her he said, 'For God's sake, woman, put me out of my misery. Will you marry me or not?'

'On one condition,' whispered Justine as she gazed down into his eyes.

'Which is?' his grip tightened on her thighs.

'That you take me back to Javea for

our honeymoon.'

'I can't see any problem with that,' he replied allowing her to slip through his arms until her feet touched the ground again, 'maybe the owners of the Casa Rafael would like someone to guard their property again.'

THE END